KLAVSTORE:
Massacre at Atlanta

A novel by

LUKE DE MARTIS

Translated by

JACOPO ROSSI LUCATTINI

CHILL

The sensation you feel when you lie naked in bed, caressed by the blanket is of absolute freedom and lightness. It is so, especially when at your side you see a beautiful girl who is naked as well, resting after having spent a whole night getting it on. Nivor Stullenbird used to know this feeling pretty well, but he was not accustomed to it. Maybe you can simply never get accustomed to things like that, and each and every time you remember the good feelings you had the very first time.

Stullenbird's bedroom occupied the southeast corner of the mini-apartment that the blue party had arranged for him. The apartment itself was located inside the alchemical research base in Atlanta.

It seemed that time had stopped, and everything looked somehow enchanted in that cold, icy semi-darkness.

«Are you awake?» the girl asked.

«Yes. Just now» he answered in a voice made rough by sleep

«Do you know what time it is?»

«I guess… something like five in the morning. We have a few more hours to rest»

«You know, I've been thinking about Dalen… I'm actually not sure if it was a dream. Anyway, it occurred to me that this is the place where you used to make love to her»

«It used to be one of several places" the 17 year old replied as he stretched.

«Nivor…»

«What is it?»

«Dalen confided to me that she wanted to ask you something… and honestly, I'm wondering the very same thing myself.»

He sighed «Go ahead, say it»

«Why have you choosen to have sex? I mean… the worldly path and all that stuff. At the Blue Party, that's a very unusual thing»

Nivor seemed to be thinking about it. He lifted a hand and stroked his chin.

«That's a good question. I used to tell myself, in the early days, that I had to take the chance… Yeah I should do it before I died. Life is short, and you got some things you have to try… Savvy?»

Liadra —this is the name of the girl— nodded.

«However, after Dalen I had other chances, then again and again. I honestly lost count of the number of girls I've been fucking»

«You're a lucky guy, Nivor»

«Lucky?» he chuckled. «It didn't took me a long time to realize I was what they call the "alpha male", and that every single woman would want to get laid by me. There was a time when I thought I could do anything»

«You have an easy life»

«That's the fucking thing. People fumfer and chat, so that by now everyone knows who I am and what I do —including my brother. By now everyone keep avoiding me like the plague, and I'm considered the worst of the worst. Scum. People hate me, Liadra»

As he spoke these words, Nivor's tone became increasingly hysterical and resigned.

«I haven't choosen to live this life, Liadra.» he continued «If I had a choice now, between being what I am and being some random loser, I would choose the latter option»

«Why should you give up a life of pleasure and freedom? You're never assigned any tasks, you have this little place all for yourself, you have a lot of fun…»

«But at what cost? These are the very reasons why people hate me. I have seen their eyes. There's such a menacing venom in them. By now I keep doing this way to forget those looks. But it ain't working.»

THREE DAYS LATER, 8:30 AM

«I'VE LOST MY PATIENCE WITH YOU!» Wakendos shouted behind the luxurious wooden desk in his office. On the other side, Nivor Stullenbird was listening.

«I used to be sure, every damn time, that you had gotten your head on straight!!!»

Nivor remained silent with his head down.

«How many chances have I been giving you, huh? HOW MANY?!»

Nivor dared not raise his head. He had never seen Wakendos —his supervisor— so angry. And that wasn't because Wakendos used to cool keeping silent, in the contrary. No: Nivor had really crossed all lines.

«Many,» the boy muttered,

«From the diplomatic meeting to the seaside vacation, passing through the volleyball games and all the free rides. You've had many opportunities to demonstrate decent behavior, and yet...[raising his voice] IT ALWAYS ENDS IN THE SAME DIRTY WAY!!!» He took a few seconds of pause, just enough time for a breath.

«Tell me, do you understand or not, that you represent an entity? You can't start doing filthy stuff left, right and centre. What's wrong with your hormones? Nobody does what you do! Nobody acts like you do! In the whole base!»

«Maybe» Nivor whispered «That's what I want»

«What's that supposed to mean?»

«Just that maybe I like to have sex and be considered a pervert. Then again, it's the only thing I'm good at.»

Wakendos' eyes almost popped out of his head. His hand began to vibrate incessantly, and he pulled his glasses down.

«Listen to me, and listen carefully, Nivor. Listen very carefully, because this is the very first time in my life that I'm saying such words»

He inhaled. Then he continued, speaking in an equally calm and threatening tone.

«You are a filthy depraved pervert. You are a worm. In your whole life, have you done *even one good thing*? What is your goal, huh? Sleeping with as many girls as you can?»

«WHAT IF?» Nivor shouted with sudden courage.

«OK. I've never done this way, but you don't leave me... alternatives» Wakendos hissed. Then he grabbed a paper and handed it to Nivor.

«In a couple of weeks at most, you're going to Antarctica. Do you know what that means? That it's just you and a sea of ice. No people, no internet, no… nothing. You'll see that the cold will do you good»

Nivor didn't have time to vomit loud all the many ramblings he was about to say, because suddenly the office door slammed open. A woman in her sixties entered the room. She was very tall and thin, and had a bony face and severe traits. She was Mrs. Woltk, someone whom Nivor knew only by sight, having passed her in the hallways a few times. But he knew that she was the chief secretary of the entire base.

«Eugeny, we need to talk urgently...» she paused noticing young Nivor «In private» she added.

«I was just forgetting, all the time you're here you'll be eating at the canteen like the rest of us. Now go have breakfast!»

Nivor took leave of his supervisor in a strangely composed and silent manner, head-down and with a thousand-mile stare. In effect, it was so early in the morning, and he had already received such a heavy insult — and from the man who was supposed to take care of him. Moreover, he was sure that in the canteen he would have to suffer some more. He was probably a little angry, but he felt mostly very sad.

Only when the two adults heard the door close and Nivor's footsteps getting farther and farther away did Woltk speak.

«Nivor is getting out of hand» she said.

«I know, I've just told him off. Before long he will be transferred»

«Not that Nivor, his brother... Aedostul»

«Ah...» Wakendos became aware that Nivor Aedostul, Stullenbird's twin, had caused far more trouble than his namesake.
The atmosphere suddenly became tense and serious.

«What has that psychopath done this time?»

«A letter addressed to him arrived this morning. Apparently, he has founded a party, called Darkblue. Part of it are the usual knowns, including Alkisatt, Doistoj, and Zinvess.»

«We had been doing everything we could to keep them apart!»

«Apparently it's not a problem for them. I'm particularly worried about the profiles of two girls… a Suzanne Dob from Nordent and a certain Daijchean»

«Let me guess... they're two fanatics, aren't they?»

«The worst possible ones. See Eugeny, that's not all I came to talk to you about. A lot of strange things have been happening lately»

«Like what?»

«Yesterday in the park two guys were handing out extremist flyers. I've had reports from the laundry room of suits they've never seen before. There is movement in the basement late at night, and some of the other Nivor's comrades have been seen tinkering with computers. I am sure there is a common denominator on all this»

«How can you be sure?»

«Tomorrow the sentence will be declared for those wretches who raped and killed our poor Dalen"

«I know. I would sentence them to death»

«The imbalance that has been created is becoming more and more blatant every day… we used to think we could control it, but we were wrong. The other Nivor is up to something and it's not just about us. I am unofficially getting reports of unusual movements from the other bases and even from the city as well»

Wakendos breathed deeply. «What are you trying to tell me?»

«I have a very bad feeling. A very definite one»

«I must confess that I have it too. But I thought it was because of the impending snowstorm»

«There is a tension so thick you could cut it with a knife. I'm sure of it Eugeny, something terrible is about to happen!»

AT THE CANTEEN

The welcome the base members gave Nivor Stullenbird could not have been more glacial. As soon as they saw him, everyone in the canteen lowered their tone of voice and started staring at him as if he were an alien.

Although he was aware of this, he forced himself to smile and look serene, even though inside he felt like he would have liked to sink from discomfort.

Anyway, he took the tray with the bowls and two pieces of plastic cutlery, then waited patiently for his turn. When the worker administering the rations —which consisted of a croissant, four slices of jam toast and a glass of fruit juice— he looked at Nivor suspiciously. He decided to ask for his base membership card, because he was certain he had never seen him there before.

Even though Nivor was an extraordinarily social and outgoing guy, no one seemed to be willing to let him sit at their table, so that he had to sit at a small table at the back of the room, where no one was having their meal.

Having no one to talk to, he focused his attention on the radio newspaper in the background. The reporter was talking about a large area of low pressure coming from the ocean, which would hit the East Coast, reaching Atlanta. He then warned the salt spreaders that there would be heavy snowfall, so that probably many roads would be unusable.

Nivor opened the single-serving portion of jam with a knife, and was about to spread it on the toasts, when he saw a boy approaching him. It was Aykol, a technician who used to work together with Dalen.

«You got guts showing up here» he told him in a cold tone.

«Excuse me?» asked Nivor confused

«We know you have a kitchenette reserved for you on the third floor. So I am wondering… or rather we all are wondering, what are you doing here? Do you want to point out how nice it is to be able to choose between having breakfast in your own private space or with the rabble? There is also the chance that you are looking for the next bitch… pardon me, girl to sleep with»

«See, here's another hypothesis for you» Nivor hissed through clenched teeth «maybe Wakendos sent me here to punish me»

«Ah, so being here is a punishment? We must have done some terrible deeds then, since we have breakfast, lunch and dinner here every single day»

At this point, Nivor got really nervous and suddenly stood up

«I ain't chosen all this!»

«Of course not. You are the perfect guy, the hero every single girl longs for» the technician replied to him, heedless of the fact that Nivor was holding part of his shirt «You were born with better genes than ours. No need to claim it, you are rightfully entitled to it»

«What part of "I ain't chosen all this" don't you understand?»

«Funny you should answer me like that, because I have met your brother.
A great speaker, to be honest. He was gracious enough to explain a
concepts or two to me… about the world and technology… and even about
people like you».

«Ok. Now it's all clear. Let me guess, that fucking bullshitter explained to
you about how the Blue Party has to let go of its ethics and how humans
have been loosing all purpose»

Aykol firmly grabbed Nivor's elbow holding his shirt.

«But most importantly, he explained to me the meaning of the word
inefficiency, and you know what? You immediately came to my mind.
After a lot of thought, I realized he was right. I am proud to say that I am
now a DB»

No one had ever heard that word, including Nivor.

«You're a *what*?»

«Something you and those like you will soon learn to fear»

Nivor let go of the shirt of the… he certainly was not a friend. Whatever
he was, Aykol walked out of the canteen with a spontaneous smile and a
snake-like look. Nivor did not stay in the canteen a second longer than
necessary and hurried up the uphill path —his quarters were located on the
third floor, while the canteen was on the ground floor. A few steps from
the exit, however, he realized he had stepped on a paper.

He bent down to pick it up and examined it carefully: a uniform blue
background, with a white stripe on the left side and two black ones close to
each other on the right. There was nothing written on it. He turned the
paper over and found the same symbol.

He then looked up in front of him. The corridor was covered in these
papers.

Few people used to know that Liadra Tloss, one of Nivor Stullenbird's "close" friends, had an aunt, Kaijha, who used to be one of the greatest humanistic alchemists of her time. She was sitting on the couches in the lounge while outside the window overlooking the tracks, a violent thunderstorm was flooding the entire station. No wonder her train was late.

Besides her, only five other passengers were there —just a few had the right to be there. They were spending their time fiddling with their microcomputers or listening to the news on the giant 56" screen on the wall —as in the case of two young women in their thirties.

The new channel on the screen was broadcasting a live report on the Relis trial, as the judges would have declared the final sentence the next day at 5 PM.

«I hope they give them the death penalty,» commented one of the two women.

«If I had the power, I'd bring them back to life just to kill them again,» replied the other.

«Some people simply have no dignity… they are scum! Why should we waste a cell for individuals like them? Consider what they've put us through: the least we can do is let them starve and freeze to death»

«If they don't get killed, there's no justice in this world. I swear I'll go there and give them a piece of my mind! Either way this is the last time I'm voting Blue»

«Me too, for sure. A guy insisted on giving me an interesting flyer for a new party. I think he called it dak...darkblue or something like that»

«I met two of them in the park. I thought it was a two-bit clique, but it looks like they're branching out. I want to see what they're doing in the future though. I have a feeling we'll be hearing from them soon.»

Kaijha Tloss kept listening to the conversation in patient silence. The longer the two women went on talking, the more concerned she looked. Most of the time, she stared at the blue poster the young woman was holding.

«I beg your pardon,» she finally said. «Would you let me take a look at that flyer please?»

«No problem»

She was about to thank the woman, when she was taken aback by the electoral points on that flyer.

The Darkblues are born!

Dear citizens, we are at the gates of a new era, the blue era.

The limited vision of those who have made ethics their blinders and the abyss of ignorance of those who indulge in their most bestial nature, are about to end! We are about to witness the beginning of a future of strength and stability dominated by an ideology that humanity has never seen before! Our points are:

- *Erasing all ethical-moral technological constraints*
- *Using and making available the highest level state-of-the-art technology*
- *Contrasting the fallacious nature of mankind*
- *Making life pure hell for all those who stand in the way of mankind's progress*
- *Regaining the respect and honor that mankind has been loosing*

Together, we shall build a wonderful future!
N. Aedostul

When Liadra's aunt finished reading the manifesto, her expression was so distraught that they could have locked her up in a mental asylum. She carefully examined the back of the flyer as well. She could not have known it, but there was depicted exactly the same flag that Stullenbird had seen on the paper in Atlanta. She handed the flyer back to the young woman without saying a word.

«If these *Darkblue* become important, they'll have my vote,» she commented.

AT STULLENBIRD'S PLACE, AGAIN

Shortly after three o'clock, Nivor was minding his own business at the place where he lived, when suddenly all the electrical equipment went off before his eyes. He feared it could be a base-wide power outage: it was difficult, because there were two redundant generators in the underground floors, but still possible. So he decided to go outside and check. Strangely enough, the corridor lights were on as usual. It was a metallic noise that brought his attention to his left: just in time to notice a figure running away and disappearing into another corridor.

About ten steps away, Nivor noticed an open plastic panel just above the floor, no larger than a dozen inches. Not far from it, were a screwdriver and electrician's pliers. Peering inside the panel, he saw a myriad of wires. Only a few well-chosen ones had been severed, however: those that powered his small apartment. Nivor closed the panel, making no attempt to reconnect the wires, —not because he did not feel able to, nor because he was afraid of the shocks.

So in the cold, in the dark and with the rain… or maybe it would be more correct to say the storm, which was becoming more and more intense over all Atlanta, Nivor put himself on the ground in front of the balcony and observed the frequent lightnings. No sound other than the thunders and the rustle of the rain could be heard.

He began to think about all the things that had been happening to him over the past two months. Maybe the others were right to call him a pervert, and so far no exceptional talent had emerged in the disciplines that mattered in his world. All he had was a gorgeous body, good skill in sports… and a certain natural ability. He had no interest in alchemical, technological or spiritual disciplines. He had achieved everything with minimal effort to the chagrin of those who, he had to admit, were far more talented than himself —and went unnoticed.

After all those insults people had been throwing at him, he began to insult himself in turn. He was becoming convinced that he was useless, that he had no purpose and on top of that the world hated his guts. Something Wakendos said to him came back to his mind, a sentence about purpose.

What was his? He realized that he had never asked himself this question, and yet if he had done nothing about it, his destiny could be just one. Nothing other than to become a crook, to get drunk and have fun every night, then once he would became an adult he would have got settled somehow thanks to the party, perhaps in the assembly workshops, or in the factories, or wherever someone physically strong could be needed. In other words, he would be condemned to a repetitive existence made of disgusting things, only to survive, like an animal. And after his death, no one would have been remembering him. He would have done what anyone else could do. He would be a mere insignificant bolt in a bridge.

He then tried to empathize with those who had treated him so poorly, and to understand why they would do so. How was it possible that a superficial person who never showed a love of knowledge or talents of any kind like him had exclusive privileges such as an apartment of his own —while other technicians had to make do with dormitories? Not to mention that most days he had to do absolutely nothing, since diplomatic representatives were rarely used.

And what about his sexual issues? The vast majority of boys his age had yet to have their first kiss, and party affiliation usually made time go up.

He, on the other hand, had already done with girls everything he could think of and his partners… he could not even count them all.

He acknowledged he had a strange feeling, calm and somewhat cold. As if anything he could do…did not matter. The nice and pleasant things, eating and sex included, seemed to be grey and sterile to him, as if they had lost all color… in other words, he had no desire to do anything. Nivor Stullenbird had begun his downfall into depression.

Someone knocked on his door. However, he did not get up to open it. The door was ajar anyway, so the person outside entered the room without asking permission. It was a girl. She was not very tall and a little chubby, and she was wearing a tech suit. She was Liadra. With the lights off, the only thing she could see was an unidentified boulder in front of the balcony.

«Nivor… Are you here?»

«Hi Liadra» he told her flatly.

«Hey Nivor, what are you doing in this darkness…» She tried to flip the light switch, but nothing happened. She kept repeating the process two or three more times to no avail. «What's wrong with the lights? Did they go out? They look blown out»

«Someone has sabotaged my power. I should have seen this coming»

The girl knew on the fly that something was wrong with Nivor. His tone of voice was strangely cold. Almost as cold as his brother's.
«You sound… strange. Is everything okay?»

«No. Don't worry, though. Take it easy. Is there anything I can do for you?»

For a moment, it seemed that Liadra desired to investigate further, but she could not hold back the anger she was feeling.

«Those bastard bitches!» she shrieked. «Earlier, when I came back to the dorm… someone wrote "slut" on my bed»

«I see. I'm sorry»

The girl glossed over Nivor's quirks «Hey Nivor, maybe you have some spare blankets I could borrow, haven't you?»

«Check in the closet to your right, I should have an extra spare»

Fortunately technicians like Liadra always carried an LED flashlight in their back pocket. She turned it on and opened the door to Nivor's closet. It was relatively tidy, at least in upper shelves. On the bottom one there were an umbrella and some rackets, weights and other sports stuff; in the middle shelves, a box with scrap metal and computer parts, and the first aid kit next to it. In the upper shelves, clothes that Nivor used very rarely, and on the last one, a white blanket with blue flowers embroidered.

The girl stood on her tiptoes and stretched her arms as much as she could, and eventually the blanket fell on her head. It was really heavy, almost like a comforter. While she was trying to fold it, out of the corner of her eye she glanced at Nivor, who had not moved an inch.

«Is… is everything okay?» she asked while fumbling with the blanket

«No»

«Would you like to talk about it?»

«No»

Liadra placed the blanket on Nivor's coffee table, then walked over to the balcony.

Nivor was lying on the ground with his back to the glass.

«Let me see if I can guess. They treated you badly, didn't they?» she asked as she crouched down

«Yeah»

«You probably won't care, but it's happening to me as well. My friends —
and *they* were real sluts until recently—, have suddenly awakened and
become puritanical» Liadra chose not to tell Nivor the whole story,
especially that some of the harassment she was undergoing was due only
to the fact that she knew him.

«The blanket issue is only the latest of many encroachments.»

«Okay,» Nivor said without looking up

«Should I be using an expression my aunt loves, I'd say we have here an
elephant in the room. Do you know what that means?»

«No»

«It means there's a thorny, embarrassing issue in front of everyone's eyes,
but no one wants to talk about it. Dalen's death has changed the game,
Niv»

«Could you please not talk about her?» he implored in a pained voice.

Finally, the girl sighed «What I'm trying to get you to understand… is that
things are going wrong for me too. I'm surprised that a boy with such a
strong character as your are has already given up»

«That's what I'd ask myself if I were you»

«Nivor...» said the girl, now extremely serious, «Why do you think these
terrible things are happening to us?»

A voice-over answered her question. A woman had been listening to the
conversation from outside at the door, and now said to her «It's because the
balance has been broken, Sweetie»

They both turned around. A woman was there. She looked incredibly like Liadra, but was twice her age. Finally, Kaijha Tloss had arrived in Atlanta. The storm had gotten so bad that even the cabs were not running, so she had to walk. The pouring rain had broken her umbrella and thoroughly soaked everything she was wearing.

«Auntie! What are you doing here?» said Liandra, quickly turning her expression into a smile.

«I have a conference in Ragdoll tomorrow afternoon. I took the opportunity to see how my little niece is doing.»

For an instant, the place glowed with a bluish light, and shortly thereafter a thunder rattled the entire building.

«It's a great surprise to see you here, auntie»

«Unfortunately it seems that things are worse around here than I imagined»

«You know auntie, someone wrote…» she was interrupted by her aunt «The guard already told me what happened»

The place was dark, and so the two could not see the expression of Liadra's aunt, but she was visibly *terrified*.

«Nivor, since this place is yours, can we all sit at the table? I need to talk to you guys. It's important»

«Okay»

The teens stood up, while the adult had already sat down. Nivor and Liadra sat on one side of the table, and Kaijha on the other, opposite her niece. In the very moment they were sitting at the table, they heard the rain getting even more intense, and another noisy thunderclap followed moments later. Aunt and niece looked intently into each other's eyes.

«When you were a little girl, your mother and I used to tell you that you had two moms, me and her. Do you remember that?»

«Auntie... could you please not say such things before Nivor?»

Actually, he seemed to be lost in his own world, not paying much attention.

«Don't be afraid to look like less of a woman, there's nothing wrong with that. I was saying… I have sworn to treat you as a daughter. I would never wish your harm»

«Are you about to ask me something painful, auntie?»

«I would like you to come with me. Along with your friend if you like, he has to handle a lot more trouble than you. Before I came up here, I spoke to Wakendos and Woltk, and they completely agree with me»

«Do you want us to attend a lecture of yours or something like that, auntie?»

«I want to take you as far away from here as possible and have you stay there»

«So it is a transfer!» she exclaimed, in a voice that conveyed all her indignation.

«No. It is an evacuation» Liadra did not like that word at all.

«What? And why!?»

«Listen to me, you both are no longer children. It's only fair that you should know. You are in danger here, real danger. For your own protection, the sooner you leave this place, the better»

«Auntie… has there been any alchemical disaster? Like twenty-five years ago?»

«No, nothing like that. This is a totally human danger»

«Can you elaborate a bit?» Liadra shouted.

Kaijha turned her gaze to Nivor. «Listen kid, you and I have never met before, but from what I've heard about you, I'm pretty sure you're not involved in this. So I'm asking you, and please answer me truthfully, do you have any information whatsoever about your brother?»

«I don't know» he replied «We don't talk much. He hangs out in the basement floors with his friends all the time. You can go there if you're looking for him»

«Nivor has seen better days» said Liadra, trying to find some funny side of the situation.

«Ok, see Liadra. You've always been a smart girl. Some things are hard to explain to those who don't know the human alchemical structure. However you must have noticed for sure that something doesn't add up.»

At that moment the girl remembered of several things from the last times: the bullying she and Nivor were experiencing, the party laws becoming more stringent, the extraordinary technological leap forward that had been taking place, the village fairs being cancelled one after another, and the fact that everyone was acting strangely.

«I don't know what you're referring to, Auntie»

 «The course of events has been changed. You must have figured that out, haven't you?»

The girl, albeit confused, nodded «I was talking to Nivor about this earlier. A tragedy has turned the tide»

«To summarize as much as possible, let's say that a certain force is becoming more and more powerful. A force that comes from Nivor's brother and from his friends»

A dull rumble was heard throughout the building. To inexperienced ears, it might have sounded like a thunder. But it was not.

«Rather take them away!»

«There are others, I'm fear. I read a Darkblue manifesto this morning»

Nivor looked up. He had heard that word before.

«Who are these Darkblues?» Liadra asked.

«They were born from the fusion of two entities. One is what used to be known as the "extremist movement" —and here we find Aedostul, Nivor's brother. The other is the anti-sex league, run by two girls who are constantly making trouble for the alchemists: Michelle Suzanne Dob and Jancamille Daijchean»

«So what?»

«This is a deadly combination. There's never been a precedent for something so frightening»

«Aykol is one of them» muttered Nivor, still staring down «I saw him earlier today in the canteen. It was not a good meeting»

«Aykol?» repeated Liadra in a hysterical tone.

«He's always been a weirdo… in the sense that he lives in his own world. What's changed in the meantime?»

«I don't know. But he was very cold and self-confident, as if he had suddenly gained power,» Nivor replied

«This doesn't surprise me at all. See guys, the situation has turned upside down, and those who used to be popular and happy should pay attention to what used to be for them obvious and familiar. The humanist alchemists are on high alert, including me»

For the first time since they had been talking, Nivor raised his head, but did not dare look the woman in the eye «You know, I've been feeling weird for a while now»

«Weird in what way?» the woman asked with some reservation

«Like I am the loser now. But that's nothing… the things I used to enjoy have become boring, devoid of any purpose. The world seems to be gray and colorless to me. Inside me, I can feel a great calm, an emptiness that is the only thing that makes me feel good»

«My dear boy» she replied in a very sad way «You just described depression. It couldn't have come at a worse time, given the situation. I must ask you guys again. Come away with me, far away from here»

«But… to go where?» Nivor asked very calmly «If the world is really fucked, no place is safe, is it?»

The alchemist breathed very calmly; Nivor was absolutely right.

«If you hurry up and pack your stuff, you can take the train with me. Most of them have been cancelled due to bad weather»

«I'm staying with Nivor» her niece replied «Unity is strength, and I don't want to leave him in this condition with those bastards around»

«You are kind Lid, but you should leave with your aunt»

«Only if you come too»

«I'm not in the condition to do so»

«Then I'll stay here»

"You're acting like children!» Kaijha shouted «The threat here is extremely real, and by the time you regret staying, it will be too late»

«That may be so, but Nivor is my friend»

At that point, the woman sighed deeply. Then, she picked up her purse and placed it on the coffee table. She rummaged through it a bit and extracted two wads of cash.

«Are you crazy, Auntie?» Liadra's was stunned, when the woman handed her one. Nivor had not even paid attention to it.

«I won't take no for an answer on this,»

Liadra examined the block of money. It had to be at least three thousand crowns! Her aunt did not look satisfied, and continued to rummage through her purse. With both hands, she pulled out a handful of small bars of pure gold, 50 grams each.

«Just in case the money doesn't work out,» she commented.

«Auntie, are you expecting a coup or what?»

Liadra had no way of knowing that those would be famous last words.

BASEMENT TAPES

The basement of the Atlanta Diplomatic and Research Station looked like a big parking lot. The walls on either side and the ceiling were painted blank white, and there were only harsh neon tubes serving as lighting. On the ground, a rather crumbling bitumen floor. To the right, was a long lab table with boxes on it. The temperature was absolutely freezing.

There was a tripod with a video camera, accurately placed so that the three boys present could be filmed full-length. On the left, was Aykol, the short and freckled technician who did not get along so well with Liadra. In the middle, was Nivor Aedostul, Stullenbird's brother. He looked a lot like him, but he was actually two inches taller and a little thinner, although he had a handsome physique as well. His face was absolutely not inferior to his brother's: shiny black hair of medium length, dull blue eyes, a smooth nose, full lips and a jaw perfectly in sync with his upper teeth.

The third boy, was Doistoj Nees, a middle ground between the others in both height and appearance.

The three of them were all dressed the same way: they wore black boots that covered half of their legs, dark pants with a belt and hoodies sweatshirts. There was something written on the hoodies: "make war, not love", "nemesys" and "this is the future". Each of them had a long black Matrix-style jacket reaching more or less to the knees.

Each of them had a special code name in the darkblue circles. Aykol was nicknamed Archangel, after the nickname he used on the net. Aedostul was the "kommander", because of his character. Doistoj perfectly represented the stereotype of the mad scientist, so that he had received the nickname "Stein" —the final part of Frankenstein.

Aykol-Archangel headed for the tripod and fiddled with the video camera. After setting resolution, lighting and contrast, he pressed the red button to start recording. It was a pretty simple digital camera, and first few moments of the recorded file captured nothing but Aykol coming back into line with the others.

«Is it recording?» Stein asked. Archangel nodded

«All right, chaps. Let us commence by introducing ourselves. Who are we?»

«We are the darkblues!» the two on either side of Aedostul shouted with one voice. Fortunately, they were far below ground, and no one could hear them.

«And what shall we do in a couple of days?» Continued the kommander

«We shall change world history!»

At that point, Aedostul stared menacingly at the camera.

«Ye may bet we shall» he hissed. «For too long mankind hath been subjugated by revolting beasts of no talent, of whom my own brother is a perfect specimen. But that is about to change. In the new era, we shall restore dignity to the world and lead it to a better future»

«The revenge of the DBs will come like a bucket of icy water» Aykol-Archangel continued «It shall be so strong, that ye shall not even realize what hath been happening»

«I cannot wait for it to happen» Stein said «At last, those who have a sincere love for progress shall have a free hand to create whatever they desire»

«The world is full of useless rats» Archangel resumed.

«The future belongeth to us. Before long, we shall prove it to you»

Kommander stared at the camera with a calm expression. He had an almost squinting look and a sly smile.

«Ye cannot imagine how fulfilled do I feel right now. Your world…» he raised his arm and pointed it at the camera «Your world shall end by our hand! We are the ones who shall bring forth the dawn of a new age»

«I can already imagine what the idiots here in Atlanta shall say» Archangel commented. Then he bent down a bit, trying to assume an expression as ridiculous as possible, and started to imitate Wakendos «You used to be such brilliant guys… why did you choose the extremist path? You could have done a lot of good things!» then he burst out laughing.

«We have no intention to use our intellect to do good for these baboons, fatty»

They all laughed. A cold, husky, purely evil laugh.

After a while, Archangel continued facing the camera, this time extremely seriously «I am carrying so much hate inside, I would erase you all. I do not mean "kill you", I actually mean "erase you". Blow you off the face of the planet»

In the meantime, Stein had disappeared from the frame. He returned holding a rectangular elongated box. Given the way he was holding it, there had to be something very heavy inside, probably made out of metal.

«Well, I guess we shall have to make do» he said.

«Ye disgust us, ye filthy animals, ye bawling, blasphemous, incharitable dogs!» Aedostul concluded.

ENEMIES COLD AS ICE

Over the course of the night, the rain turned to snow and hail. Thanks to the harsh winds, low pressure, and the fact that the sky had remained overcast for the entire day, the temperature reached 16°F. From midnight onwards, the snow began to abundantly cover the streets. By two in the morning, the hail had condensed to the point of forming blocks of ice the size of tennis balls that devastated entire cities, destroying antennas, cars, and windows.

The extraordinary low-pressure wind sent these weapons made of ice with devastating force towards the poor, unlucky targets.

Exceptionally, the emergency management organization declared a curfew on the entire Eastern part of the American continent. This did not help prevent the multiplication of fatal accidents on the streets and code red injuries to the poor unfortunates who tried to return to their homes, getting instead an ice ball on the head that literally knocked them out.

In areas where hail and snow did not arrive, the rain flooded making entire regions uninhabitable. Meteorologists estimated volumes as high as 400 millimeters in just a few hours. Streets became long rivers flowing between buildings, and low floors flooded in no time.

The most popular symbol of this devastation was probably a photo that immediately became viral on the net: it pictured some escalators in a shopping mall leading directly into a sea of grayish water. The administrative and research base in Atlanta, however, had double glasses on all the windows —to norm of law— exactly to face situations like this. The only issue, was that the satellite antennas on the roof were damaged by the strong winds, de facto interrupting communications with the outside. Anyway, there were still the underground cables connected to a large router, which had recently undergone maintenance.

Throughout the base, at least three night watchmen had the task to be awake and patrol the building. Not exactly an easy task, given its size.

That night, one of them was Sien Lovut, a young man in his thirties who had never stood out in anything. Sien was the classic guy next door: he had brushed hair, a long and thick moustache with a goatee. Unfortunately, he had recently gotten quite overweight, but he had promised himself to go on a diet.

The routes that the night watchmen used make, were completely random. However, it had been specified in their official instructions that they had to "avoid going over the same area". At that moment, he was passing through a cozy and luxurious elaborate wooden hallway, where the offices of the base's senior management staff were located.

The structure of the base's hallways was extraordinarily complex, constituting almost labyrinthine, so that it was easy to pop up, curve around, and head somewhere else.

After yet another turn, he saw something quite unusual in the distance: a steel banger with something on it. Sien was not able to get a better sense of what it was until he got closer.

About ten meters away from the target, he could better understand the nature of what he had seen. A young man was standing on top of a steel ladder. He had both his hands shoved into a small hatch in the ceiling, and was clearly intent on tinkering with something. A closer look, and Sien could immediately realize that the hatch had been made in correspondence with a simple electrical outlet. Evidently, whatever "object" the boy was fiddling with, had been improperly plugged in.

«Who are you and what are you doing?» the watchman asked.

The boy lowered his head toward the Sien, who was shining a flashlight at him. For a moment, he looked vaguely panicked, then made an effort to simulate a calm and composed attitude.

«My name is Doistoj Nees, I am a technician» so far no lies.

«Hey shorty, do you have any idea what time it is?»

«Yes. It's past three o'clock» Doistoj-Stein answered. He had been waiting for that time, sure that no one would have been around.

«You technicians sure are having a hard time. Are they making you work this late?»

«Well, I'm here,» Stein replied, trying to skip the question.

«Have you finished doing… whatever you were doing?»

«Yeah, I just triggered the bo… I mean, anyway, I'm done»

«Glad to hear it. Have you seen what a weather we have?»

«No doubt about it…» Stein hissed «With the hail and rain, it's going to be hard to get around»

«You're telling me kid, I feel trapped like a mouse in here. The base is also in a high place, for a while no one can get in or out»

Doistoj smiled sinisterly.

Nivor Stullenbird could not sleep. He had too many bad thoughts in his head. Moreover, that strange feeling did not want to go away. Everything had become bland and he simply could not find happiness in anything. He kept standing in the hallway, observing the disastrous weather situation. He began to wish for this to end as soon as possible.

THE LAST PIECE OF THE PUZZLE

Every person in the world who woke up that Tuesday had only one thing on their mind: the final verdict in the Relis trial. Understandably, everyone was interested in the verdict, for one reason or another. Blue Party sympathizers, on the one hand, felt the need that the wrongdoers were punished properly. On the other hand, outcasts and people with rebellious or anarchic tendencies were interested in seeing what would happen if they went too far. Various foreign countries observed the event as if it were a lunar landing. The trial was broadcast live around the world and translated into 70 languages.

The day had started out as a cold and frosty Tuesday. A misty fog pervaded everything. Soon the Eastern States had to deal with the damage caused by the hurricane. Over the course of the day the situation calmed down a little bit, but the meteorologists kept affirming that in the following days there would come more extreme weather phenomena.

Everything in Atlanta was covered in snow, and residents were amazed to see the landscape tinged with white.

Everyone was experiencing a strong anxiety about the process. People living in neighborhoods that had suffered the most severe damages, had the chance to pass the time counting the precise extent of the damages. Some people started to repair what they could, but the estimates of the appraisers and the civil engineers showed that to fix that slaughter would have cost not less than one billion crowns.

To make matters worse, the thick layer of snow covering the roads was making it absolutely impossible to rely on any means of wheeled transport, as cars and trucks got mired in the snow. The only hope to get rid of the problem, was to wait for midday, hoping that the sun would melt the snow.

In the afternoon, the whole continent became deserted, even the areas not affected by the storms. Not a single open store could be find, nor a single car heading anywhere could be spotted. Everything looked like hypnotized and waiting for something to happen.
The Ragdoll base could really appear to be a dwarf, when compared to other larger ones, such as Radget-Erun or Atlanta. However, with its two floors it met all the needs of the city. The scientific activities that it hosted were limited in number and variety, and its administrators showed a more marked tendency towards bureaucracy than its larger counterparts'. The few technicians who were employed there, were just enough to cover the ordinary administration of the city.

The base was conveniently equipped with a theater in the back, where the politicians in visit could held rallies and the senior department officers could hold meetings on security topics.

The theater had a capacity of 800 seats, and was all painted blue except for the red seats. The stage was made of wood, and included a long table, fully equipped with microphones for several speakers.

Kaijha Tloss had arrived at about ten o'clock. In the morning, the weather was more clement. Anyway, at her arrival she was met by two diplomats who escorted her all the way from the station to the base.

The announcer introduced her as the humanist alchemist who had written the book "*The Elephant in the Room*" and one of the most talented women in her field.

«Thank you all» she said in response to the warm applause raising from the public. The theater, anyway, was only half full, because everyone who had the chance had preferred to watch the live broadcast of the trial.

«I am fully aware that many people judge humanistic alchemy as the most useless branch of science. Usually people pay more attention to technological alchemy, because it is the one that gives life to our most modern equipment». She paused to look at the audience in front of her.

«Humanistic alchemy, however, is far from being purely speculative. If you look it up in any dictionary, you will find that humanistic alchemy is defined as that science, which studies the alchemical structure of man. In other words... It is the scientific discipline closest to take into consideration the concept of *soul*»

«This is a very loose definition, I know. However, it is useful to help us understand what we are talking about. The alchemical body of man is something that is halfway between soul and psyche»

«Every person is urged and driven by two opposing forces: order and chaos. Chaos is responsible for those instinctive and non-rational behaviors, while order is the force that fuels our logical behaviors»

«Of course, these two opposite polarities would be untenable if they did not counteract each other. If there were only chaos, goodbye civilization… we would all come back to be beasts! If there were only order, we would become cold automata that do only what is asked them, like computers do»

«Fortunately, these two forces are in balance with each other… or at least they should be… as a result, we can say that we live in a compromise, where they are present in a moderate form»

«In modern society, there are such things as amusement parks, if we need to unplug. I'm free to make love to whoever I want without accounting to anyone. I can smoke a joint if I want to have a funny time. These things we're used to are part of chaos. On the other hand, we have the police to protect us from evildoers. We have reached a certain level of technology,

and our overall organization allows us to be comfortable. This is all thanks
to the polarity that I have called order»

«This is the balance we have achieved, and this is the invisible harmony,
on which our society is based… and it is wonderful and fascinating… as
long as things are going well»

«Two years ago, a group of thoughtless people tried to take the polarity I
have called chaos to extremes. You all know what I'm talking about. At
that time, violence dominated the streets, crime had reached unbelievable
levels, the only law was that of the strongest. Then a fact happened. A girl
was raped. She used to work at the Atlanta Base, where I was yesterday. I
have a niece there. It could have happened to her»

«Luckily, the Dreamwalker came into play. An extreme remedy for an
equally extreme evil. As we know, Relis dropped down dead and we are
still here»

Then the woman's voice became almost a whisper, though amplified by the
microphone. «However, such a risky maneuver created a huge imbalance
of forces that completely changed the cards on the table»

«We thought we could cushion this imbalance. Remember, for every
action there is an equal and opposite reaction. In these days, we have been
realizing not only that this is so, but also that we are breeding devils in our
bosoms. And they will sooner or later come to light»

At that point, Tloss examined one by one the puzzled and confused faces
of the people who constituted her audience.

«The balance has changed. We can all sense it. Think about the last weeks.
We know that a strange chain of events has been activated. No one has
understood exactly what it is, but we all have the feeling that we are
missing something, as if it were right under our noses.»

At that point, the people present began to reflect. Some even began to
suspect that what they had been listening to was not just a bunch of
nonsense: on the contrary, it conveyed some truth.

These thoughts were short-lived, however. All vanished, when a young man in the audience suddenly shouted. He had just read in an online newspaper the sentence delivered for the Relis case.

«I can't believe it!» he shouted, unconcerned that everyone was listening.

«Those scumbags got off with five years of community service!»

A sudden buzz erupted through the room.

«It's an injustice!» commented one woman

«Those judges are incompetent!»

«They were probably bribed!»

«Those crooks got off with only having to serve five years as garbage collectors!»

«How can you be such a do-gooder with scum like that?»

«If I had been one of the judges, I would have given them the death penalty, not just 5 damn years!»

The presenter grabbed the microphone and invited those present to calm down, without succeeding. In fact, the comments became increasingly audible and violent.

Kaijha Tloss became pale, and seemed to almost faint.

«We're fucking screwed» she finally said.

At that moment, she was probably the only one to fully understand that the chain of disaster was now complete. Now nothing in the world would have prevented what was about to happen.

THE ELEPHANT IN THE ROOM

Imagine that every single citizen had a favorite team, and that that team had just won the World Cup. Not even in that case, you would witness such a confusion, like the one that followed the ruling. Screams of discouragement and swearing echoed through the now deserted streets. Several people were in such need to let off steam so badly, that they started breaking just the first thing at hand. An elderly man threw a glass at the television, with the only result to shatter both.

All that noise, however, turned to deafening silence over about one hour.

Not that the anger and fury had suddenly disappeared, quite the contrary. These feelings had flowed into something else, something cold and fearsome. Something that no one dared talk about.

However, sometimes a silence can say what words could not. When the businesses reopened for the afternoon shift, people were treating each other with great coldness and indifference, interacting very little beyond what was strictly necessary to conduct businesses.

Everywhere: on the streets, in bars and pubs, in supermarkets, in restaurants. Every and each place became the scene of a surreal, unnatural silence.

Such un unnatural silence did not go unnoticed by anyone —no one at all. Towards dusk, a mother and her son were in a supermarket restocking their supplies for the next few days. They were standing in front of a freezer in the yogurt section.

«Mom, can I ask you a question?» the child suddenly said. He was very short and could not have been more than eight years old, to be generous. The woman nodded.

«Why is everyone so quiet?» the little boy asked, trying to be as clear as possible.

«Don't talk about it» the mother replied with a certain indifference.

«Why not?»

«Because you must not!»

A chilling phrase, yet filled with truth. That evening, guests at the senior clubs as well as kids intent wandering in the streets, everyone continued to live in this strange, surreal silence. No one dared bring up the topic, yet everyone knew what was going on —and why. People were simply being polite and friendly with each other, although it was clear that it was a cold and fake friendliness.

Who could have imagined that a silence would be scarier than any words?

In the bases, including the one in Atlanta, dinner was served as usual, but with great caution. They were aware that a single spark would be enough to start a violent raging fire. Only at that very moment people were getting to understand something. After all, bringing together all those very different young guys, from excellent diplomats like Nivor to electronics students who spent their days on books… maybe it was not exactly a good idea. The very fact that boys like Nivor were the girls' favorites while the others were left high and dry, would have been enough to portend a great potential for discord.

That evening, the neon tubes seemed to be whiter and harsher than usual. At times, their low electronic hum could be heard, as the various tenants of the base ate in strict silence. If someone had something to say, they said it in a whisper or under a their breath.

Woltk was observing. She thought that among those boys there certainly were the extremists willing to come to power by any means necessary. They were mixed together with the others, most probably they had common faces. The normal and the extremists, everyone was breathing the same air. Probably he had even talked to them, and surely they had given *normal* answers, as if nothing had happened to them.

Sooner or later, however, all knots come to the comb. Nothing could stop or change what was going to happen. Their destiny, in some way, had already been written.

In the meantime, the rain resumed in full swing, and intense thunderstorms followed one another throughout the night. They lasted all the next day.

IT SHOULD NOT HAVE BEEN LIKE THIS

Apparently, it was not different from any other Wednesday. But it was "*the*" Wednesday. The day, in which world history would change forever. Any situation is the result of an intricate tangle of cause-and-effect events, so everything that had happened before, had led to this day.

Nivor was to leave the Atlanta base a dozen days after that Wednesday. At the turn of November and December, there was to be a major technology exposition —as was customary every three years. That year promised to be very fruitful for the humanist alchemists, who seemed to have discovered new connections between the various human alchemical centers, called chakras. Tloss would have been delighted to work with them. Liadra would complete her term a year later. After that, she could have worked for large companies in computer industry.

Some short films released by the Blue Party heralded a new efficient operating system, codenamed "ocean".

There were all the necessary ingredients for toy companies to be able to release new, colorful alchemical toys for children —who seemed to have regained interest in the Goest-Berg stuff from twenty-five years earlier.

The Blue Party had promised to experiment with transmitting electricity through the ionosphere in case of a new electoral victory.

One of the many possibilities of destiny would have led to this and much more. It would have not absolutely been a bad scenario. But it was too late. None of this would have taken place.

The Atlanta base had a recording room on the second floor. That morning the recording of the classic hymn *Nearer, My God, to Thee* was scheduled. The music instructor assembled the boys' choir and finished the recording under noon.

The lunch was consumed without incidents of any kind as well.

The base's "yellow tracksuits" —that is, the athletes— had planned to play a football game in the back courtyard. However, the snow had started to fall in full force again, making it unthinkable to even set foot outside the building. The athletes did not give up, and put on their yellow tracksuits anyway, waiting in the canteen for the snow to stop —which it did not.

Given the extremely boring situation, the trainees and young people —like Liadra— were given the afternoon off, so that both girls and boys spent time relaxing in their dormitories and having a break from the hustle and bustle of their everyday life.

At five o'clock in the afternoon, suddenly a mysterious bang echoed through the building, but no one could tell what it was. Almost everyone agreed that it must have been thunder. Not at all. In fact, it has been a minor "technical mishap" concerning what the DBs were planning to do that night.

Finally, they managed to record one last tape, just before they passed the point of no return. The location was the usual empty basement with pillars at regular intervals. The three young men were standing in line. They were visibly tense. Stein was sipping an energy drink. Before long he would need his strength. All his strength.

«Well folks» Aedostul began «This is our last tape before the big event. We have synchronized with the other bases, and the time has been set at 7:30 tonight. Before long we shall see some great things, and the blue era shall finally be born. So far, everything hath happened as planned. The trial hath been a disgraceful farce, and the whole world is a tinderbox ready to explode. We are the spark»

The three boys remained silent for about ten seconds.

«To converse about other matters, chaps» Stullenbird's brother continued «What role do ye want to have in the new era?»

«I want to be the Minister of the Interior» Aykol said

«Alas, Archangel! That position hath already been taken by Dob» Aedostul answered him.

«Then I want to have the Ministry of Public Utilities»

«We shall see what can be done. And thou, Stein?»

«I do not care for the name of the position. I want to have labs of my own»

«Thou shalt. Well, chaps, the clock is ticking, and we have a mickle to do. If ye like to go over the plan, all the better»

«We know the plan, Komm» Stein muttered between sips of his drink.

«Rereading a plan hath never hurt anyone» Aedostul said.

«However, ye should be acting with autonomy… I mean, chaps, this is our night. We shall be the undisputed protagonists who shall gloriously enter the history books. We few, we happy few, band of brothers. But above all we shall have a good time»

«Please remember. We can only do this once, after which it shall no longer be possible. Thus… Do your best»

«Ah the Devil fetch me! I shall certainly enjoy myself!» Archangel hissed as he stroked his rifle.

«And the funny thing is, we are going to be idols» Stein added.

«Ye know what I have been thinking, chaps?» said Aedostul «This is like a baptism, for us as much as for the DBs. Something that marks the end of everything that used to be so far and the beginning of a new era»

«A rite of passage!» Archangel specified

«Essentially a rite of passage *for this planet.*»

RED WRITINGS

Warning: from here on out, things get really bad.

If you do not wish to read disturbing passages, please go no further.

The three boys stood proudly, wearing their black coats and long boots. They had their backs to the two large entrance doors of the base, in the stark white entrance hall. Their expression was extraordinarily theatrical: they were looking up in a defiant tone, chest out and back straight.

In the entire base, there was only one person who could legally bear arms: the security guard standing in the next room.

With confident steps that echoed throughout the place, they reached the gatehouse. The guard was minding his own business, casually reading a magazine.

When he saw them, he immediately understood that there was something far beyond the ordinary going on.

«What are you three doing here? Why are you dressed like that?»

Unceremoniously, Aedostul pulled out the large, heavy rifle behind him. Vincent —that was the guard's name—, stood paralyzed in his confusion.

PAM-PAM-PAM

Hylon's body fell to the ground in a neat and composed manner, like a building that had just been demolished.

The three young men went on without saying a word. Ahead, there was a small lobby that marked the full-scale entrance to the base. Aedostul went up the stairs that were right in front of it, Stein turned left, and Archangel turned right, heading to the canteen.

*** *** ***

With the antennas out of sync, the only way the base could communicate with the outside world was through the phone line. At 7:32 PM, the old landline phone at Wakendos began to ring. The number visible on the seven-segment display showed the Nordent area code.

«Hello, this is Atlanta Municipal Base, I'm the human resources manager» he answered in an annoyed tone.

The guy on the other end of the phone was out of breath and speaking without much clarity. «H-hello… my name is Jehij… I am a technician at Nordent. Two girls… one of them shot…»

«I beg your pardon sir?» Wakendos asked confused.

«I couldn't see their faces… I fled to the first place I could find… so I thought…»

At one point the boy stopped talking.

«WHAT? YOU!? WHAT ARE YOU DOING HERE… WHAT ARE YOU GOING TO DO WITH THAT THING!?»

Through the phone, Wakendos heard a dull bang.

He was stunned for a while, then resumed speaking.

«Hello? Hello!? Nordent, what's going on there!?»

On the other side, the girl approached the phone while Wakendos continued to shout.

«Who's there?» the girl asked.

«Hello? Whom am I speaking to!?» Wakendos yelled.

«Is this Atlanta?» the girl asked in a remarkably cold manner.

«Yes, it is! But what the heck is happening there? What was that noise!? Whoever you are, tell me how the situation is!» There was a long pause across the phone line, then the girl asked very quietly,

«I am pretty stunned it doth not seem rude to thee to hang up the phone like that»

«Hang up the phone? What the heck are you talking about…»

KABOOM!!! A huge explosion devastated all the executive offices. Wakendos was buried in the debris. He had hung up the phone.

*** *** ***

Liadra was cutting out some origami with her friends when she heard the bang, which rattled the building like a bat hitting a pole.

«What the hell was that?» she asked.

«It didn't sound like thunder,» observed one of her friends.

«It's definitely the males messing around in the canteen»

«I don't know about you, but I'm going to go check it out. Just in case» Liadra said as she got to her feet. Liadra walked out and went down the the stairs on the right side, thus saving herself by a hair.

Almost at the same time, in fact, Doistoj "Stein" Nees arrived at that floor, coming from the stairs on the opposite side of the corridor, so that the two did not cross each other.

He already had his rifle at pelvis level. He was holding it with both hands.

Meanwhile, the girls in the dormitory were oblivious to all that was going on.

«Do you think we should keep her company?» Valejye asked

«Nah, let that slut fend for herself» Sushanna replied.

«Anyway, I'm going out too. I need to get some air» Valejye added stretching as she approached the door.

She was just about to close it back, when the twenty girls in the dormitory heard a loud noise, like a dry bang. The only thing they could make out, was that it came from the corridor. They turned around and looked at the door, but all they saw was Valejye slumped against it. The door itself was stained red, as if someone had thrown a paint balloon at it.

«SOMEONE SHOT HER!» Sushanna shouted. She was the only one that had seen everything.

Panic broke out in the dormitory. The girls screamed at the top of their lungs, hoping that someone would come to their aid. The only result they achieved, however, was that they made Stein even more furious.

«What is going on here!?» Stein said, as he scanned the room in front of him.

The girls immediately ducked behind the beds as soon as they saw him and continued screaming.

To end the infernal din, Stein fired a shot that broke a neon tube on the ceiling. Somehow this maneuver had the desired results, but so simply because the girls were now too terrified and trembling to keep screaming.

Liadra had flattened herself behind the stairs, trying as hard as she could to keep the noise down. She had not seen what had happened, but she had heard everything. First, she had to run; second, to call for help.

«'Tis about time for you get quiet and be silent. Is it so hard for you lasses?» Stein said. Then in a shockingly high-pitched voice he took to imitating them.

«Ye lasses are always whining about everything. "Ohh, the makeup, ohh, the shoes, ohh love, blah, blah blah!"»

«Do ye see what happens then? When ye have a real, serious reason to raise your voice, ye are speechless!»

Given that the front row had no other beds to hide them, two girls had stepped aside into a corner. Stein pointed his rifle at them.

BANG, BANG.

The first girl was shot right in the heart, and died immediately; the second in the stomach, and would bleed to death in a few minutes.

Stein intended to have some more fun with the remaining girls, who had taken to moaning continuously and ungainly, as they kept hugging whatever might give them some comfort.

«Let us see… now who shall I kill?»

He then began to chant in a somehow merry and joyous way, jumping from bed to bed. He pointed to a girl crouched behind a gray bed.

«Shalt thou be the next one to die?»

The girl did not have time to look at her assailant, who had already jumped to the opposite side, this time pointing a girl behind a yellow one.

«Or shall it be thee?» and in the meantime he had already fluttered to another side.

He caught sight of three girls holding each other together, albeit very shakily.

«Ye three! How about a nice little trip to the next world?»

Finally, he came to Sushanna. He stood in front of her, while the girl pushed herself into the wall as much as she could.

«Art thou still a maiden?» He asked.

The girl kept trembling, and positioned her lips and tongue to pronounce a NO.

BANG.

Sushanna was hit in the middle of the forehead.

Almost simultaneously with the blow, Stein heard some sort of rustling behind him. He turned immediately to prevent someone from attacking him.

It was actually a frightened, trembling girl standing on the opposite bed. Stein watched her carefully, then smiled at her. «But thou certainly art, 'tis written all over thy face» he said in a friendly tone.

Then he took the moment to reload from the belt of ammunition at his sides. «Go ahead! Go to the basement, thou shalt be safe there. If the Kommander or Archangel make a fuss, say I sent thee there.»

The girl did not move, however. «What art thou still doing here? Take a deep breath, then start the marathon running!»

The girl did not wait for him to repeat his words anymore. She got up and ran away in silence.

*** *** ***

In the meantime, Liadra was running at full speed. She had lost the ability to reason clearly and her actions were dictated solely by her instinct of survival. At a certain point in her running down the stairs, she saw a human figure approaching her. Without thinking twice she stopped to go back. However, she suddenly realized who it was.

It was a tall, slender woman with grey hair. It was Woltk. Noticing Liadra's agitation, she hastened to speak.

«Don't worry, little one, the situation is under control. Just, no one go near the management sector»

«IT DOES NOT SEEM TO BE UNDER CONTROL TO ME!»

«What the hell are you talking about, girl?»

«There's a fucking guy upstairs happily shooting at my friends!»

Under normal circumstances, Woltk would have taken for granted without hesitation that the girl was mocking her. After seeing her office swept away by a flash of white light, however, she realized that was just the least of the trouble.

«Was anyone hurt?» the woman hurried to ask.

«He's shooting! Many, and they're not wounded, they're fucking dead!»

Woltk's face became pale, and she had begun to tremble as well.

«Good Lord… I didn't expect it like this… and so soon»

«DID YOU KNOW ABOUT THAT?»

«If I had known I would have evacuated the base, wouldn't I?»

Liadra sighed fearfully.

«See little one, it's nothing. Tell me, are there any others? Shooters, I mean»

«In the underage dormitory only one, but I think so. I had the impression he was coordinated with others, probably downstairs»

«Okay» Then the adult, though she knew her little, rested her hands on Liadra's shoulders.

«It's okay Sweetie. It's nothing. Now that we know, this little game is much easier. See, we need to get as many people as possible to safety, you and I. Do you want to give me a hand?»

Liadra swallowed, then made to nod. The general secretary of the base pulled a necklace from around her neck, at the end of which was a small notched steel tube, no longer than two inches.

«Find any of the fire sensors. You will see that there is a hole. Insert this key, and the alarm will ring. Then run as far away from here as you can»

«Why me?»

«Because nobody else can do it. Let's show the men what women are capable of» And lastly, she kissed the girl on her forehead.

*** *** ***

In a parallel corridor, on that very floor, Nivor Aedostul was walking slowly, confidently and eerily toward his target, firing on sight at anyone who stood before him.

Two orderlies and an electrician were killed for merely standing in his way.

«I am coming for thee» he growled. «When I get there, I am going to slaughter thee like a pig, thou damned and lustful mountain goat. 'Tis time for a showdown!»

Then he saw two children playing tag.

This is red writing, no more words are needed.

*** *** ***

Liadra was running wildly all over the floor, glancing down every corridor, either to look out for an attacker or to check for a fire alarm. Never before had it seemed to her that things are always in the way, when you don't need them —but when you need them, you never found them.

In her heart, she was praying that that could be just a horrible nightmare that would end as soon as possible. As she approached a corridor she heard gunshots here and there. The further she went, the louder they became. She noticed that she was strangely close to where Nivor Stullenbird, her friend, had his apartment.

Every cloud has a silver lining; in the corridor where she had snuck to escape the threat, was a laundry supply store with a smoke sensor.

She ran as fast as she could to reach it, with long strides. She risked slipping at more than one point, but finally reached her goal.

She stood in front of a long red column with a bell at the apex.

At a height of three feet, was the classic red button in a white box to set off the alarm.

That button would have rung the bell up there and those nearby, but probably not in the entire base.

But she knew that in her hand she had something more powerful.

Beneath the white box, was an almost invisible hole. Liadra gripped the carved steel tube and inserted it into the slot. She could perceive some resistance, and it made unpleasant sounds like it was rusty inside. However, it had gripped perfectly. She turned the key to the right. That single turn seemed to take an eternity. As the key returned to its starting position, however, she could clearly hear a click.

In a split second, almost immediately, the corridor was tinged with red.

The glass cones under the ceiling lit up, and a dazzling red one-way light began to spin inside them, creating a beam of light that went from one side to the other.

A high-pitched, deafening siren came out of the generators and a pre-recorded female voice began to repeat:

«General alarm! Leave the building immediately! This is not a drill. General alarm! Leave the building immediately This is not a drill...»

In some strange irony, this had the effect of calming Liadra down. She realized she still had her backpack with the money and gold her aunt had given her. All she had to do at that point, was to get out of there alive…

No. There was still one person missing.

*** *** ***

Nivor Aedostul could already see "that" door in the distance. Perhaps he also noticed the panel where Stein had done his work with the electricity.

Suddenly, the headlights lit up there too, and a red light hid every other color that was present, casting long, sinister shadows. The siren and the voice immediately reached maximum volume.

«What's new now?» he growled.

No harm done. If the rat had even tried to stick his nose out of his nest, he would have seen it. He was a goner.

Aedostul was already looking forward to the moment when he would take care of that problem, he had his mouth watering.

So, when he arrived at the door, he charged at it with all the strength he had.

49

«I'M COMING TO KILL THEE, THOU FILTHY ANIMAL, THOU PIGEON-LIVERED!"

The impact of Aedostul's body slamming against the door made the whole structure shake. Infuriated like a bull, he took a running start and brought down all the energy he had on the door —including the weight of his body which was no small thing. The blow literally smashed the wall where the lock was located. The door was not open yet, but it was about to give way.

At that point, Aedostul got really nervous and started to growl and roar. He called upon all the anger, viciousness, evilness, cruelty and hatred he had, and charged at the door one more time.

"I'VE HAD ENOUGH OF YOU, YOU FILTHY RAT, I AM SICK OF THEE!"

SBAM. The door had been knocked down.

*** *** ***

Archangel bursted into the canteen kicking the door open. Since it was almost dinner time, it was relatively full of people. All the various categories of people were standing just blissfully talking or sipping beer.

The canteen had tables of four, six, eight and twelve seats, gradually becoming more and more rectangular in shape. Those damn people were having a happy and carefree time there. Too much so. But what caught his attention more than anything else, were the yellow jumpsuits he spotted with some sporadic frequency.

Without giving them a chance to see that he had entered with an assault rifle, Archangel pointed it in front of him, then turning from left to right he opened fire across the room.

The screams that followed were a hellish roar for Aykol-Archangel

«SHUT UP!» He screamed in a wail, emptying all the breath into his lungs.

It would have been too good for him if everyone had kept quiet. However, some wretch who had not realized what had happened was overcome by instinct, when he saw that ugly man in black with a rifle in his hand.

After getting the attention of the entire room, Archangel's plans changed. If he had previously planned to randomly shoot anyone he did not like, he now had a target.

«EVERYONE WEARING A YELLOW TRACKSUIT STAND UP!»

«YE SPORTSMEN, STAND UP!» But of course, even if they were stupid and ignorant, they did not stand up.

«FINE, THEN I'LL COME TO FIND YOU!»

The canteen had a small bathroom on the opposite side of the entrance. In that very moment, a guy in a yellow tracksuit came out of it. A heavyset guy with considerable muscle.

«Who called us?» he asked confused.

BANG, BANG, BANG, BANG!

Of the four shots fired by Archangel, only two hit him.
The boy fell to the ground, but was still breathing.

Archangel approached furiously like a train, always keeping by the wall — he thought the people present might get up to fight him. Then he reached his victim.

«Stop…» he pleaded «Don't kill me…»

«Too late»

Archangel killed the boy

51

The others in the room murmured in shock.

«Quiet, quiet! Everyone's turn cometh sooner or later!»

An office clerk took up speaking, trembling and frightened.

«What's the point of all this? Is this a kidnapping? A robbery?»

«'Tis the consequence of the filth ye have been up to, ye cowards, ye unable worms!» Aykol-Archangel stated with some confidence.

Then he headed furiously towards a table with several boys in yellow suits underneath. There were six of them in all. The others were hidden around the room.

Aykol-Archangel's walk was strange: with a hunched back, a grin from cheek to cheek, his teeth clenched and his rifle down.

The yellowsuits, and sportsmen more generally, were a living representation of what DBs loathed most: A bottomless morass of ignorance, headbangers proud of their stupidity, thinking only of sex, drugs and getting drunk. From the DBs' point of view, there were no more repugnant people. No one was capable of unleashing such extraordinarily violent impulses in them.

BANG. BANG.

The first shot hit the boy on his shoulder. The second one was fatal.

«One down»

The boys stood side by side and stared helplessly at Aykol.

He pointed his rifle at another one of them.

BANG.

Before continuing with the others Aykol took the opportunity to snicker, proud of his feat.

«What happened to your manhood? See how ye tremble, ye three-inch fools, ye beasts. Because that's what ye are, animals. Ye act like animals, ye are animals… and I shall slaughter you like animals.»

One of them swallowed nervously. He knew he had to say what he was chewing in his mind. He was not sure if it would have been enough to save his life. Had he not tried, he was sure he would have died.

«I… I know you,» he said almost under his breath.

Aykol-Archangel immediately pointed his rifle at him.

«I beg thy pardon?»

He wanted to analyze that face before deciding whether to possibly take him out.

That was the classic square-faced big guy with a bulging jaw.

«You're that weirdo who always keeps quiet, aren't you?. Your name is Aykol, and you work in the alchemical industry»

«How dost thou know who I am, thou filthy worm?»

«You had a fight with our bro Nivor the other day»

«Ah, him. I am pretty sure his brother hath found him by now. But now let's take care of us! I would beat thee, but I would infect my hands…»

BANG

*** *** ***

Liadra had the impression that the corridors of the base had turned into an inferno. With those rotating lights and screaming sirens, it seemed to her that she was in a dream. She had a strange feeling, comparable perhaps to a drop in blood pressure. In fact, she felt she was about to faint. Soon the world began to spin around her, but she had to make it. She had to reach Nivor.

She had entered the last corridor, by now…

Nivor's place was very close. The closer she got, however, the more she noticed a detail; the door was not there.

When she got close enough to see it, she became aware that she was facing the worst-case scenario.

Nivor's door had literally been ripped from the wall, and was now lying on the floor.
She did not even dare to imagine what strength could have accomplished such a feat.

Everything in there was in complete disarray. Apparently, someone had rushed in, not bothering to bump into things or throw anything on the floor. Then, they had left for the rooms, always violently slamming the doors. Finally —observing the carnage in there— they had opened the cabinets, moved the sofa, overturned the bed, broken the glass in the balcony and even shot the toilet bowl. At that point both Liadra and whoever had preceded her came to the same conclusion.

Nivor was not there.

Then, hoping not to do anything in vain, she rummaged through the drawers in his room, grabbed some clean clothes, his papers, the money and the gold her aunt had given him.

*** *** ***

Just before the world descended into total hell, the Ragdoll base janitor passed by the quarters where Kaijha Tloss was staying. Having knocked at the door and hearing no response, she concluded that the alchemist should be elsewhere.

She was in no way prepared for seeing what she found there. The woman was hanging from the ceiling with an electric cord around her neck, knotted to the fan.

Kaijha Tloss had taken her life.

THE THREE BECOME FOUR

The canteen soon began to resemble a large slaughterhouse. Everywhere the eye rested, there was a body or a pool of blood.

He had shot in total 14 people, 2 of whom were still alive, albeit just barely.

Aykol was convinced he had taken out all the yellow suits, when he glimpsed a small, imperceptible movement.

And moreover, in a part of the room where he had already been.

He immediately ran to see what was going on.

What he saw was heartbreaking. One of the yellow-suited guys had got hit in the chest, where a hole was radiating blood all around. Though, he was dragging himself out of the canteen crawling with the help of his arms — he had also been hit in the leg. He was spending all his energies left trying to get to safety, and in doing so had created a red trail on the floor, like a slug with slime.

Aykol-Archangel, on the other hand, could not bear this affront.

«How darest thou drag thyself out after I shot thee!» he yelled at him.

The boy gave him one last look. He was sad and resigned.

«THOU SHALT NOT FOOL ME! IF I HAVE DECIDED THAT THOU DIE, THOU DIEST, DOST THOU UNDERSTAND?»

Another boy died, after a grueling drag towards life.

It had been enough for Archangel to calm down. Thinking he had completed his "task" at the canteen, he got ready to go somewhere else, leaving those who had not bothered him still alive. He had almost left the room, when a voice called him back.

«Hey, you shooter guy, get over here!»

Archangel instantly stopped. Whoever had called him, had not at all the manly, raw voice of the yellowsuits, so he wondered who the hell had the nerve to challenge him.

With hasty step, he headed for the small table from where he had perceived the voice, reaching in a short time. He saw was a pale, dry-faced boy with a confetti-thrower's physique.

«What dost thou want?» he asked disinterestedly.

«You happened to forget two of them,» the little boy replied with narrowed eyes.

«I beg they pardon?» Archangel was actually quite confused.

Then the boy pointed to a small table in the back there, well hided and protected by bags, trays and other stuff.

«There. There are two other people in yellow tracksuits. I don't care if you shoot me too, it's just not fair that you skipped them»

Archangel was initially in disbelief. Anyway, he headed right where the boy had pointed and demolished that little makeshift fortress.

There were two sportsmen holding each other like sissies.

At that point Archangel came back to the boy. He was smiling.

«What's thy name?»

«Aeron Tsan»

«Aeron. Why did you tell me that?»

Aeron kept silent for a moment. All the pranks they use to played on him in Atlanta, the intimidation, the bullying, all came to his mind. He thought about how they seemed to be magically luckier than him, how they used to be and socially active, while he was always sidelined.

«They're different from me,» he finally said.

By then, Archangel had totally calmed down. He had now a peaceful expression.

«Get up, Aeron. Come by my side»

The little guy was shaking conspicuously. However, he got closer to the assassin.

Archangel gave him his hand. Together they approached the two guys under the small table.

They seemed to be on the verge of tears.

«I don't want to watch you shoot him,» Aeron pointed out.

«I shan't be the one doing it.»

In a bold and daring move, Archangel slipped off the strap of the rifle hanging from him, and placed it against Aeron's head. Suddenly the boy felt a heavy weight on his neck. Then Archangel put the rifle in a horizontal position.

«Put your hand here,» he said, resting his fingers on a spot about five inches before the end of the barrel.

Aeron did so without saying a word.

«Now, with the other hand hold this thing from the right, putting your finger under the lever»

Aeron was handling the rifle correctly. Archangel backed away, aware that at this point he was as much a target as the two nearby.

«Do it. Thour't one of us»

Aeron looked like he was suffering greatly. But finally, he thought, he was in a position of power against those who had always overpowered him. Finding the courage to tighten his index finger was difficult, but eventually, with a bit of effort —more psychological than due to actual resistance of the lever— he was able to pull the trigger.

The sportsman on the left was shot in the neck

«That's for a good start,» Archangel said, sincerely impressed,

«Now you shouldest...»

There a few quick movements. The guy on the right suddenly tried to escape. He was hunted down by Archangel, however.

«No, no, thou shan't escape!» he said, as he was grabbing his suit.

However, the guy was actually much stronger than Archangel and tried to punch him, only to miss him.

BANG

Aeron shooted him in his lower his back. He survived.

The sportsman literally kneeled at the feet of Archangel, who stepped back. At that point, Aeron pointed his rifle toward his head, and shooted twice.

BANG. BANG.

He finished what he had started

«Well done, little man. I knew thou wert one of us»

Aeron covered his eyes with his hand, incredulous. He could not believe what he had just done. He had a rifle hanging from his shoulder, and he was responsible for the deaths of two people. But he himself had revealed their presence, so he had probably always desired to. He just did not know that he would have done it himself.

«See Aeron, dost thou want to join us? Thou didst not lack for hatred, for sure! And with a little training…»

«Why have I done that?» Aeron whispered.

At that point, Archangel knelt down and wiped the tears from the boy's face with his fingers.

«See, thou saidst it. They are different from thee, and that's perfectly true. 'Twas thee who pointed out their existence to me, even though thou knewest what I would have done at that point. Thou wantedst to. I'm not so different from thee, I just got tired of rabble like that having everything and us having nothing»

«I'm into alchemy» Aeron said «Designing alchemical stuff is my life's purpose, but no one cares»

«The DBs do. I do. In the new era, thou shalt have the place you deserve, I give thee my word. Not only shan't we be punished in any way when we leave here, but the world shall consider us heroes. Thou shalt be able to be part of the government, if you just desire to be»

«I… I want the things I do to become important»

«They shall. We DBs shall rule the world one day. And with "we", I mean also people like you, who don't let these scumbags walk all over them»

«Are you going to make my creations spread everywhere?»

«Yes. I promise»

«I… I'm beginning to understand why you're shooting. These guys wouldn't do any good anyway»

Archangel seemed to be genuinely pleased «Thou soundst just like a DB, dost thou know?»

«Are you sure nothing bad will happen to me if I ally myself with you?»

Archangel nodded, but did not give it too much thought. His attention was on the strange movements he had just noticed to take place between the soda machine and the juice dispenser.

He lowered himself a little to reach Aeron's ear.

«Now let us pretend we're leaving. Hold my game,» he whispered softly, so that only Aeron could hear those words.

«Well, let us get out of here now, there is nothing to do anymore!» Aykol pronounced clearly. In the meantime, he was approaching the dispenser, walking very slowly

«Considering what I have been doing here, I don't want to set foot in here again»

SBAM.

Camouflaged behind a plant among various accessories was another boy in a yellow tracksuit. Taken by surprise, he moved frantically. So a few items fell out of his pocket: two condoms, a bag of weed and a Zippo lighter with the male and female symbols crossed. This boy was pretty different from the others. If there was one ethnic group the DBs were particularly upset with, in fact, it was Hispanics. This because —according to Aedostul and his comrades— they were the most depraved. Exactly like that boy, with his unmistakably Latino features, mulatto skin, stocky physique and exotic look.

In an instant, everything Archangel hated was showed to him. He felt a visceral, spontaneous hatred. He gritted his teeth and his face grimaced.

«AERON, COME HERE!»

The boy shuddered at hearing such a threatening tone. So he ran to reach Archangel as soon as possible.

He slowed down as soon as he saw the big guy all cowering and staring at his rifle. Aeron did not miss a single detail, neither the two condoms, nor the bag of weed, nor the Zippo.

«Tell me. What dost thou think about what thou art seeing?» Archangel asked

«I don't know if I should say this…»

«Of course thou shouldest. In thine own words…»

«I hate him…»

At that point, Aeron, without Archangel telling him anything, was guided only by his basic instincts. He raised his rifle and pointed it at the guy.

Archangel saw him out of the corner of his eye. He pushed the rifle down with his hand, just in time.

«Hold it,» he said, «I got a better idea.»

Then he turned to the Hispanic boy.

«What's thy name, thou filthy animal?»

The guy looked scared to even open his mouth. With some effort, however, he managed to speak: «Miguel» he said in a rough voice.

«And which jungle dost thou come from?»

«I… I'm from Ecuador»

Archangel turned to Aeron. «Get his lighter» he whispered. His new "accomplice" complied without objection.

He came closer to Miguel, looking at him in contempt. He and took the Zippo, carefully avoiding to touch the condoms.

«Good» Archangel said «Now we are all going to take a walk. Me, Aeron… and thou!»

He waited for Aeron to have the guy at gunpoint again, then he ordered «Get up, thou rooting hog!»

Very slowly Miguel stood up. They noticed he had an even darker skin color than they had expected. He also had a noticeably strong ribcage.

«Now come forward, but keep staying away from us»

The three of them walked out of the canteen. Miguel was leading the way, wondering what the hell did they intend to do with him. Aeron came after him, and followed every little move he could make with his hands. From behind, Archangel was overseeing everything.

They were soon in the corridors, where the light was blinding. Archangel occasionally instructed Miguel which way to go. They kept heading west and entered a maintenance corridor.

In the middle of that space, just opposite a storage room, Archangel announced, «Kneel down, Miguel or whatever thy name is»

The Hispanic boy stared at him with a look that conveyed not so much perplexity as disquiet. Did they intend to execute him there?

«Kneel down, I said. Don't make me repeat myself»

With a lump in his throat, Miguel did as he was told. A noise was heard. Archangel had opened the door to that small, shelved storage room. When Aeron saw what he had pulled out, he immediately understood what he intended to do.

Suddenly, Miguel felt a cool liquid soaking his shoulders. The first thing he thought was something like, "Are they going to piss on me?" but he could tell from the smell that it was neither piss nor water nor anything similar.

It was an artificial, chemical odor, which he was sure he had already smelled—but he could not remember where or when. It could not be acid, otherwise it would have already caused him devastating injuries. As Archangel emptied the tin container, he was extremely pleased to notice that the yellow tracksuit had excellent absorbency. Finally, Miguel was completely drenched, and a large puddle of the liquid was at his feet.

At that point, Archangel walked away satisfied, laying the tin on the ground as well. «Aeron, give me…»

«No,» said coldly the boy. Archangel looked at him in disbelief.

«I want to do it myself» he added.

«Alright. Step away immediately though, it can be dangerous»

Aeron leaned over and extended his arm, still staying a considerable distance away. Only when he heard the "clink" sound of his Zippo opening, Miguel realized what they had thrown at him. It was gasoline.

Miguel was set on fire and burned alive until death came. It would have been a long and extremely painful death.

And while Miguel was running, screaming and wrenching in pain, the two kept watching in silence. There was nothing left of the human being he used to be. He was now simply a warm, glowing flame that walked and shone through the hallway, which soon reeked of an intense stench of barbecue meat.

The pain caused Miguel to lose consciousness shortly afterwards, when he entered a sort of coma. Even now, Archangel and Aeron did nothing to extinguish the flames, which devoured him to the last shred of skin.

At last, the handsome and attractive Ecuadorian boy who had been there before, was turned into a pile of coal, ash and soot —no more resembling a human being anymore, but just a giant burnt roast.

«Thou shouldest find a weapon of your own» Archangel told Aeron as he examined what was left of Miguel. The boy raised his face.

«Thou shalt find everything you need in the basement, including a jacket similar to mine. Chances are Stein invited more decent people down there, they need to be treated with kid gloves. The entrance is at the bottom of the base, then left. I am going back to the canteen. I need a hot chocolate»

Could you make me one as well, when I get back?»

«Of course. One last question, dost thou have a nickname thou likest?»

The little boy lifted his gaze and seemed to be thinking about it.

«A nickname, huh? That's not easy…»

«We all have one. Mine, for example, is Archangel. Upstairs there are Kommander and Stein»

«Lighning. Because of the storm…»

Archangel smiled «Lightning is a perfect nickname. In line with our ideology, eerie and mysterious. Now go.»

*** *** ***

Woltk went down the stairs as fast as she could —perhaps too fast for her no-longer-young heart, but no matter. Only one thing mattered, more than anything else: to save as many lives as possible. It did not matter if it was going to be her own loss.

She had reached the second floor. Suddenly, the walls turned from white to pink and the lights under the ceiling began to move, and the siren rang. "Good girl," she thought, "You made it."

In the distance, she saw five boys. One of them was pretty chubby. They were coming out of the library. She ran in their direction to warn them of the impending danger.

As she progressed, she noticed that the second floor —where the canteen, the library, the music room, the computer labs and other utility spaces were located—was packed with people. And immediately she realized that a mass evacuation would create too much confusion.

«STOP IMMEDIATELY!» she yelled.

The chubby boy looked at that high ranking officer coming up towards him.

«Secretary Woltk, what's going on? We heard a terrible bang earlier, but we thought it was a firecracker. But now the alarm is ringing»

«See» she said, trying not to agitate anyone «We are facing internal enemies»

«Internal enemies means that...?»

«That there are unidentified people with hostile intentions. Extremists»

The boy bulged out his eyes.

«Now answer me. How many people are there in the library?»

«I don't know exactly, ma'am» he said «thirty, one more one less»

Woltk held his breath. If they had gone out, they would have made too much of a mess and in all likelihood would have got caught. No, there was only one thing to do.

«You and your friends go back into the library. Explain to those present the situation and these rules I'm about to tell you»

«First, make sure that no one from the outside can see anything of what's going on inside. Put a sheet or coat over the small glass window. However, you always have to keep an eye on the door. Second, never, under any circumstances, make any noise. Turn off all your electronic devices if necessary

«And you, ma'am?» the boy asked.

«This is the part you won't like,» she said, as she took a key from her pants' pocket.

«I will be locking you in from the outside. It is purely for your own safety. When the troubles are over, you can come out»

Those who were outside went back into the library, and told the others about the tragic news. When no sound was heard, and the small glass window had been covered by a blue jacket, Woltk closed the entrance to the library.

Then she moved on. She had to secure more places, and she had not a moment to lose.

*** *** ***

Aeron, now nicknamed Lightning, was in a corner in the lower floors of the base to the left. Over there, he found the stairs leading down to the basement of the base. They consisted of two other floors. In the first one, there was abandoned technological stuff who knows how many years old.

It was extraordinarily cold down there, because the heating did not reach the underground area. It was the kind of cold that makes you appreciate the comfort you have, that makes you feel safe in your bed. But at that moment, the 15-year-old had a lot more on his mind.

The entrance to the second underground floor was well protected by warnings about danger of death, threatening signs, and a more poetic "ALL HOPE ABANDON, YE WHO ENTER HERE" There was something dark down there —and it was not just about the signs. Aeron was perfectly aware of the technological side of alchemy, and he was certain that the place was well charged with negative energy. Who knows how long Archangel and his comrades had been plotting down there, giving birth to the DBs, their ideology and plans. Finally, there they had planned at the table the massacre that was taking place.

At first glance, there was not much of extraordinary. Just a small library, a sea of papers and a big backlit table, similar to a billiard table. Around that table —Aeron thought— they used to discuss what to do.

Further ahead, he saw a couch, and next to it a shelf filled with various food items —most of which had already been eaten.

Next was a series of boxes. The shape of those boxes was unmistakable, many surely contained rifles.

On the opposite side, a gigantic computer, the most advanced and technological system he had ever seen. It was a strange hybrid of top-of-the-line parts and handmade stuff. Moreover, there was an alchemical material he had never seen before, dantlefin. There were lots of compounds and bottles of chemical stuff —which they had surely used to make explosives.

At the other end of that place, he saw a door leading to a room so large, that it was somehow disturbing to enter. It was the place where they used to record their tapes. Now it was completely empty, except for the supporting columns of the base. The floor was earthy, the lights were bare and harsh neons, and it was cold, very cold. He could only imagine how the DBs evolved. At first, they must have been just a clique of isolated losers with extremist ideas. Then they had become a real threat. Finally, that had turned into what they were that very night. He wondered how they had managed to conceal themselves so well, to find the time to meet down there and organize a plan in such minute detail. But most of all, he wondered how the hell the Blue Party could not notice what was happening right under their noses.

Hidden behind the wall, was a little girl about his age, with long hair and an angelic, childlike, shy face.

«I… your friend said I could stay here,» she said.

«What are you talking about? Who are you?»

«The guy who…» she hesitated, as if to hold back tears «shot up the fifth floor… he said I could stay here»

«I see» Aeron replied «Evidently you are a person of value too. That's why they left you alone»

«Did they ask you if you were a virgin too?»

«I actually am, but it was not necessary. I joined them spontaneously»

The girl looked horrified.

«Why would you join guys who are shooting? Are you crazy?»

"Actually they are a bit violent. But they are right»

"Now you are going to start killing people too?»

«I already have» he said, alluding to the two boys he had shot and Miguel.

«Then stay away from me»

«I'm not even interested in being close to you anyway. I'm just here to get some stuff»

Thus said, he headed to the corner where, hidden in a black envelope, was the fourth rifle. They had bought it in case one of the three was defective. Luckily, the DBs were used to abound in everything, so they had ordered more ammunition than they could have on them.
The rest, in effect, was there, in a backpack.

«I hope you know what you're doing,» she said.

«If you think the police are coming, know that's not going to happen. Riots are taking place all over the world. And there's too much snow. From what I understand, they are doing this just to push the government to fall»

«And at this rate, it will fall for sure» she whispered.

At that point, Aeron turned back to go where he had seen a black coat.

*** *** ***

Archangel returned to the canteen and walked over to the drink dispenser. He searched in his pocket, took out two coins and selected the button for hot chocolate. The sugar level could be set from one to five. For him, a level two was just fine, and as for the little boy… he didn't know his taste. At a guess, he set it at five. He had a funny but strange feeling coming back into that room and seeing the way it was: bodies everywhere, mess and blood. He certainly did not have OCD, but he could not stand all that mess. Finally, sitting down on a small table, he contemplated what he had accomplished.

FOG

No one had seen Nivor Stullenbird in a very long time. He had always been an impetuous and rambunctious guy used to catch everyone's attention. Since a couple of days, however, he had become a sort of ghost.

He had shut down his soul, and seemed to desire nothing more to do with the world. He was in a pitiful state, both physically and mentally.

He was on the fourth floor, lying alone in a service corridor where no one passed, with his back to a radiator a window above him, from which he could observe the copious snowfall.

In front of him, he could see nothing but the blue pajamas and white socks he was wearing. He was keeping his left leg bended and his right one stretched out. He was holding his head on his arm. In his right hand, he had a music player continuing to play the same set list of depressing hip-hop songs in his earbuds. At his side, was a half eaten candy bar.

He did not know exactly what was going on inside of himself. It was something a sea that is calm but rough at the same time. Something surrounded by fog.

*** *** ***

«Thou hast arrived. That was quick!» Archangel said as he stared at Aeron in the doorway

«Thy chocolate is on the coffee table,» he added.

After thanking him, Aeron told him what he had seen in the basement.

«There's a girl down there. I think one of your friends told her to go there.»

«Must have been Stein. Thou hast treated her well, hastn't thou?»

«I just ignored her»

«Good boy. Fix that jacket better, though, 'tis all askew»

 The little boy slipped the rifle off his back to get his outfit in order.

«May I ask you something?» he said.

«Of course»

«What's going to happen when we get out of here? I mean, I get that you're planning to rise to power… But where are we going tomorrow? What are we going to do?»

«Thou art a smart chap» Stein commented «The riots should have started by now. We have friends waiting for us at the park. We shall go over the course of the night. Once there, all we have to do is say that we set up this show to avenge the murdered lass. We shall be greeted as heroes»

«Her name was Dalen» Aeron pointed out

«Whatever. Thou shouldest not worry about that, however. Kommander Aedostul shall take care of that. He is so good with words»

«And then what?»

«All of us DBs will gather in Feedotkall to coordinate the riots. We shall wait there until both the executive and legislative branches have fallen. New elections shall be called, and we shall get our fill of votes»

 Aeron seemed to be carefully thinking about it. Suddenly, the red lights came on and the alarm began to ring.

«What happened?» he asked.

«Someone hath activated the main alarm. That needeth a key, so 'tis definitely the work of an executive officer»

Aeron looked up at the ceiling.

«Dost thou want to go upstairs and check it out? Archangel asked.

«If it's not a problem»

«I would anyway»

*** *** ***

Woltk had managed to secure two computer rooms, the music room, the alchemist's lab and eight private rooms.

She had just come out of the engineering room, after carefully explaining the situation to those present. Suddenly she saw two people dressed in black in the distance. They had what looked every bit like a firearm on their shoulders.

As quickly as she could, she dropped the key and kicked it under the door.
When the two boys saw Woltk, they quickened their pace. Archangel
whispered something in Aeron's ear, and then turned directly to Woltk.

«Good evening, ma'am chief secretary, good evening!» Archangel
shouted.

«I have not yet finished my analysis of the alchemical dispersion in the
purple energy bubble generators,» Archangel continued.

The woman showed no fear and walked over to the two.

«What do you hope to do Aykol? Who is that boy?»

«A friend of mine» he replied snickering.

«A friend who is helping you carry out a massacre?»

«Thou shouldest not be so melodramatic. I am just cleaning this place of
the human waste 'tis infested with. Thou saidest it thyself, keep thy post
clear of what thou dost not need»

«See Aykol… in broad terms I can imagine what's going on in your head.
But what you are doing is wrong, and…»

«AH, CERTAINLY! FOR SURE! WHEN I USE VIOLENCE, I AM
WRONG… BUT ALL THE OTHERS CAN MAKE FUN OF US
TECHNICIANS WHENEVER AND IN EVERY WAY THEY LIKE
IT !»

«Yes, I know technicians are often targeted, but you should have been
reporting it»

«I am tired and sick of the life I used to have, Mrs. Woltk!» Archangel
said «People like me and Aeron… I mean Lightning… we are always
treated with disdain. And yet we are the cultured ones, we are the ones

who make the world go round… we, not those mounted-bodied fools who are talked about so much!»

The woman sighed. «You can't change society, Aykol»

At that point, Archangel looked at Woltk straight in the eyes, with an evil, hate-filled gaze.

«Who hath said that?»

BANG.

Woltk, chief secretary of the base, was killed while trying to get people on the second floor to safety.

That night, Archangel and Lightning attempted to break into the halls that the woman had closed, but were unsuccessful. Everyone inside survived. In total there were 98 people.

*** *** ***

Liadra had been searching for Nivor throughout the base, without managing to find him anywhere. She had been risking a lot for him, getting closer to the three killers than she would have liked. Suddenly, she had a flash of genius. The last time she had seen Nivor, he looked very down in the dumps. So she came to the conclusion that he was hiding in a place where no one could find him.

On the fourth floor, on the west facade, there was an area that everyone considered the most unseemly and ungainly of all. Commonly known as the "scrap metal depot", it consisted of large rooms, where obsolete components, electric motors, rusty equipment and so on, were crammed.

Even the corridor was pretty rundown; its paint was falling off the walls, many of its lights were burnt out. Generally speaking, it had a staunchly neglected atmosphere.

She had been walking a long way, until she had found herself in an area of the base she had never personally seen before. Suddenly, she saw someone. In the distance, near a staircase, there was a boy in blue pajamas sitting on the floor in front of a radiator, listening to music. It was him.

She got closer to him as fast as she could. At every step, however, she could realize that there was something deeply wrong with Nivor.

Physically, it might have been him; but he certainly had nothing of the good, joyful boy she used to know.

«Nivor, I've finally found you!»

The boy lifted his head, removing one of his earbuds.

"Yeah. You found me,» he said coldly.

«We need to get out of here. I already got your stuff»

«I don't see why I would do such a thing» he replied.

«Nivor, you may not know it, but there are guys shooting around here! We have to leave if we don't want to come to a bad end»

«*If we don't want to come to a bad end*» he repeated «That's right»

«What's wrong with you?»

«I know why they started doing this. They're looking for guys like me. That's because I have no merits»

«It doesn't seem to be the right moment to talk about merit… we're in the middle of a shooting!»

«Liadra» he said slowly and softly «Please leave me here. I have no reason to leave»

»What do you mean?»

«Should I leave, I would continue to be the same awful, clueless person I've always been. I'm an ignoramus proud of his nothingness. Only now do I realize it»

At that point, Liadra placed herself on the ground next to Nivor

«You may be clueless, but I love you»

The girl came up to his face and made to kiss him, but he pulled away and put a hand there in the middle

«Please don't. I would like to be alone»

«If I leave you here, you will die»

«Why should I strive to survive? I have nothing to do in this world. It would be a waste for everyone»

Liadra now raised her voice and pulled Nivor's pajamas towards herself.

«Listen to me carefully. You are Nivor Stullenbird, the biggest screw-up and pain in the ass to ever set foot in here. The person I know would never lie here in this state or say these things. Now get dressed, and we'll get out of here»

«Well…» he said, not very convinced «Whatever»

Nivor slowly got to his feet. He looked down. He was very pale, as well as looking generally confused and neglected.

Liadra opened her backpack and handed him the clothes she had taken from his place.

Slowly Nivor put out his hand and took them.

«Turn around,» he told her,

«What?» she asked.

«I told you to turn around, I got to get changed»

«May I remind you that we had sex?»

«I don't care. Just turn around.»

Although reluctantly, Liadra did as Nivor had asked her. Only after making sure the girl's back was turned and she was not peeking, did he proceed to take off his pajama shirt.

Then she could hear the rustle of his pants being lowered. Nivor had completely gotten changed. He did not even have enough strength to put on his shoes; somehow he managed to, however.

«OK. Done,» he said.

Liadra looked at Nivor. Only then did she realize how dark the clothes he was wearing were, and how absolutely resigned his face.

«Now let's get out of here. You take the backpack»

«Do I have to?» Liadra stared into his eyes. She had her gaze higher, as he continued to have a thousand-mile stare that expressed no emotions.

«Listen, Nivor. I'm going to get you to safety, even if it means dragging you»

Then she did something; she reached out and grabbed Nivor's hand.

«Come on, we got to hurry!»

They began to run. In effect, it looked as if the girl was dragging him. She was trying to go fast; he was always lagging behind and pushing himself reluctantly. It looked like a mother taking her reluctant child to school.

But Nivor was no child; he was a six-foot-tall, 180-pound boy. So the process was not so easy.

*** *** ***

At 20.35, a message from the Prime Minister was aired on all networks, interrupting every show that was being broadcasted. The announcement seemed to be so serious and important, that it attracted a great following even on the web, becoming viral on social networks.

The Prime Minister was Winnal Erun. He used to be a chief exponent of the Blue Party. He was a moderate man in every sense of the word. Even though he was part of the "technological side", he had become increasingly less eager to explore the fields of research further beyond what was already known. As a consequence, his government had become known for having increased bureaucracy and procedures in general, both paper-based and digital ones.

He was a man in his sixties, of fair height; he had white hair and a classic inspector's mustache. While delivering his speech, he was wearing a standard politician's suit. In the background, a wooden desk and a golden curtain could be seen.

«Good evening Klavatrean people. I have just been informed about the disturbing events that are taking place. I beg those of you who are listening to excuse me, for how I will set up my message. In effect, I actually did not have time to prepare a full speech»

Then a long pause.

«The entire country is undergoing violent riots and attacks on the established order. Hundreds of protesters have gathered outside Parliament to throw Molotov cocktails and set trash cans on fire. Furthermore, several bases are being targeted by armed assailants. The exact number of people who lost their lives is currently not known. It is certain, however, that there are victims»

«There is no precedent for such a violent uprising. Things have gotten so serious, that several police stations have been targeted, as well as city halls and even government ministries. Citizens are extremely concerned, after seeing the streets filled with protesters. In certain cities, the armorers have been pelted with all kinds of objects —even clearly dangerous ones. Some of them have been rushed to hospitals»

«Many bases, just to name a few Nordent, Aurora, Cottydel, Revelso, Feedotkall and Atlanta, are currently in an unknown situation. Where law enforcement has been able to intervene…» he hesitated «They have found real carnage.»

«It is now obvious that someone lies behind these events. Under no circumstances could such tragedies have originated out of nowhere, all at once. The intentions of these dark enemies are still unknown»

Then he raised both his gaze and his voice.

«I acted as best I could to prevent them from continuing their criminal design; unfortunately, without succeeding»

«I call myself a moderate. Some people do not like the sound of that word. They mistakenly believe that being a moderate means not having the courage to go all the way. I give this word a different definition, that of knowing where to stop»

«I believe that one of the noblest limits to acknowledge yourself have, is to know when to step aside and accept that someone else will come after you»

Then he sighed.

«For this reason, on behalf of the government I represent, I intend to publicly tender my resignation in the hope that someone will succeed where I have failed»

The government had fallen

*** *** ***

The announcement had the effect of fueling up the riots, which became even more violent than they already were. Erun was seen as an incompetent who could not handle the riots, on the one hand, and washed his hands of them, on the other.

Soon, the news that the DB were responsible for what was happening spread among the crowd; immediately, their blue flag with two black bars on the right was used as a symbol of hope for a rebirth and a new social order.

A few hours before, the term "DB" was associated only with a clique of young pretenders. Over those hours, however, people began to love them: many were even inciting them to commit even more violent acts.

The opinion that people had of them at that very moment, was that they were everything the Blue Party should have been but was afraid of being.

People with a sincere love for order and technology; people ready to avenge an innocent girl raped and killed —even if it meant going against the established order. The fact that they were committing a massacre was of little importance. In effect, their targets were the so-called "socialites", who at that time were frowned upon by the masses themselves.

Soon, the protesters began to shout for new elections and the entry of DBs into parliament.

*** *** ***

«Everything goeth according to plan,» commented Nivor Aedostul, who had heard the speech over the radio. Everything that night was turning out to be an absolute success. Everything, except for that damned wretch of his brother.

Where had he gotten himself into? He could not have known he was about to be hunted, and when the alarm sounded he was already not in his quarters. Yet no one had seen him leave the building. He had to still be there.

THE ICE MAN

«Come on, you slowpoke!» Liadra urged, as Stullenbird struggled to keep up, lagging far behind. They had made their way through the maze of corridors of the base. They needed to escape, never mind face the snowstorm.

«Liadra…» he said

«What is it Nivor?»

«I may be talking nonsense, but the elevators are very old»

The girl did not understand. Had Nivor not only become depressed, but completely dumb as well?

«Yeah, so?»

«So I don't think they're interfaced with the alarm system»

«Are you suggesting we take the elevator?»

Nivor nodded.

The girl thought about it for a second.

«That's a good idea! That way we'll avoid a lot of trouble»

Suddenly, the boys stopped, making a harsh noise with their shoes, and stepped back. They had noticed a figure behind them.

«I am afraid ye'll have to rethink your plans»

It was evidently one of the three people who were shooting, since he had a black rifle on his shoulder. He had taken off his black jacket, however. He was wearing a deep blue tracksuit with black shoulders —while the elbows and sleeve outlet were white. It appeared to be a fine, soft fabric.

«RUN AWAY, NIVOR!» Liadra shouted.

«If I just notice ye are about to do something like that, I shall shoot you instantly,» the figure hissed.

«What… what do you want from us?»

«From you, ye filthy worms? Absolutely nothing»

He had a masculine, deep and calm voice, like a true orator. In another situation, Liadra would have probably asked him if he was part of the choir.

Then the guy raised his arm and pointed his finger at Nivor.

«Thou worthless sack of shit! I wish thou couldest disappear right now!»

At that point, Nivor clenched his fists and took the floor.

«Tell me why do you always take it out on me? We used to love each other when we were kids!»

«STOP! BOTH OF YOU!» Liadra shouted. Then she turned to the guy in blue.

«May I know who you are? Why are you so mad at Nivor?»

The guy chuckled, «And who might I be, thou foul bitch?»

«His brother,» he said finally.

«How can you say such words towards your own brother! What do you have for a heart, a block of ice?»

«SHUT UP! I AM SICK OF THEE, THOU STUPID LASS! I SHALL TAKE CARE OF HIM FIRST!»

«How canst thou be my brother?» said Aedostul

«How can a filthy scum like thou art have anything in common with the magnificence of what I am? THOU LUSTFUL PIG, THOU OBSCENE AND CROOKED CREATURE, THOU ART THE RANKEST COMPOUND OF VILLANOUS SMELL THAT EVER OFFENDED NOSTRIL. THOU MAKEST ME VOMIT! THOU ART NOTHING BUT A THORN IN MY SIDE!»

At that point, Liadra replied in Nivor's defense

«You have nothing superior to us!»

«Thou thinkest so, lurid bitch?»

Suddenly, Aedostul grabbed his rifle. Liadra promptly stood in front of Nivor, fearing he was going to shoot him.

But he did not. On the contrary, Aedostul slipped it off his back.

«It would be too little if I shot thee. Thou wouldst be off to the other world in no time…»

«Oh, no… I want thee to suffer. I shall take care of you… I'll be as careful as a brother can be!»

Saying so, Aedostul dropped the rifle on the ground. Then he kicked it in a way that sent it directly to the couple opposite him.

Liadra took a few steps back, while Nivor continued to look down.

«Take it,» Aedostul said.

Nivor remained still

«I TOLD THEE TO TAKE IT, THOU ANIMAL!»

Nivor swallowed nervously. Then, all trembling, he picked up the rifle a short distance away from him.

«Good boy. Now shoot me.»

Both Liadra and Nivor opened up their eyes.

«What did you say?» she blurted,

«I asked you to shoot me. Go ahead. Try to take me out»

«Do it, Nivor» Liadra said. «Either we do it or he'll slaughter us» she added

«Thou'rt smart, for a bitch» his brother replied.

Nivor had begun to tremble harder and harder.

«I don't shoot anyone» he said «Not even you»

Nivor's brother smiled with a satisfied expression.

«I should have been expecting that… thou'rt not capable of it. This is just one of the many differences between us. I had been hoping that in thy last moments thou wouldst behave decently, at least for once. What a pity»

At that point Aedostul put his hand into his right breast pocket, and pulled out an eight-inch blade knife. It was remarkably sharp, made of stainless steel and with a carbon fiber handle.

«Your partner will be the first to go bad»

BANG

To the amazement of both of them, Nivor had shot his brother.

He was certain he had hit him, so much so that Aedostul had a backward leap. Both Liadra and Nivor expected him to collapse on the ground in a pool of blood. Unexpectedly, however, he got back upright.

«Well, better late than never,» he said.

«How can you talk? I saw the bullet hit you» Liadra exclaimed in all her amazement.

«Uhmm…» Aedostul mumbled «Dost thou want to try again?»

BANG, BANG, BANG!

Nivor shot his brother three times more. Each shot hit him in the chest, puncturing his blue suit. The bullets, however, came out of him exactly as they had gone in —no blood or anything.

«That's too bad. Not very effective, is it?» he said.

«THOU COULDST HAVE A CANNON OR EVEN AN ATOMIC BOMB! THE RESULT WOULD NOT CHANGE!»

«That's not possible!» Liadra shrieked in amazement.

«Humans cannot withstand a bullet of that caliber! That is absolutely impossible!»

At that point, Aedostul came closer to the two of them, with a slow, determined, and eerie walk. Then he raised his arm and simulated a gesture, as if he were throwing a small marble at them; but there was absolutely nothing in his hand.

Instead, something strange happened. A sort of bright blue lightning was generated from the palm of his hand, illuminating the air with its iridescent silhouette. Something made of pure energy, which zigged and zagged until it reached the two of them.

Immediately, they collapsed to the ground. The electricity penetrated deep into their bodies, turning every cell into pain and almost making their hearts explode, speeding them up like crazy.

«IF THAT'S THE CASE THEY DON'T THROW LIGHTNING BOLTS FROM THEIR HANDS EITHER! BUT WHO EVER SAID I WAS A HUMAN?»

Nivor stared at his brother with eyes wide open.

«You… are a monster!»

«Look who's talking!» he replied with an icy cold chuckle.

Then he continued « Thou'rt the one who is degrading himself! Thou doest that filthy thing thou callest sex… thou'rt the one giving up thine intellect and dignity to lower thyself to the level of a beast!»

Then Nivor began to clench his fists. Even his tone of voice changed, becoming extremely serious, and sounding almost like a whisper.

«I have no idea what you've done… but you've certainly defiled your body far more than I have»

«Ha, ha, thou'rt really funny! Dost thou want to know what I have done? All right! I got rid of my old flesh and blood body, and created for myself a new alchemical one! A very complex procedure, obviously. Certainly standard Blue Party science could not have come up with it. NO! This is superior DB technology!»

«You mean you're just a projection!?» Liadra asked

«But that doesn't make any sense! Then how did you hold the rifle… how can you wear clothes?»

«AHAHA I AM NOT SO STUPID TO TELL YOU»

"I am the first of a new bloodline, my dear. Soon there will be others like me! I already have in mind what to call them: apostles. Face it: I am the evolution of mankind. I am currently the most advanced form of life on this planet! Ye lice are nothing but filthy evolutionary regurgitations that I shall sweep away»

Thus said, repeating the gesture of throwing the marble, he shot another lightning bolt at them. This time, it was much thicker in diameter, and had a color similar to indigo.

Liadra and Nivor were literally thrown into the air, falling to the ground about two meters away. They looked at each other. Both had a look full of terror and resignation. They read in each other's eyes that they knew they were about to die.

Liadra looked at Nivor one last time. She tried to see every detail of his face, which was now full of cuts, bruises and blood stains. Only at that very moment, he started to shed tears.

She reached out her hand and began to caress his face.

«See Nivor, I'm not an alchemist like my aunt… but if what he says is true, there's nothing we can do against him»

«He's just my brother, Liadra» the boy said leaning towards her.

«Your brother no longer has a body… he's no more made of flesh and blood like we do. He does not belong to biology, but to alchemy. I don't know if humans can do anything against such a creature. We certainly can't do anything in the condition we're in»

Nivor sighed.

«So this is really the way it ends. It doesn't matter. I can still feel depression inside»

The two reached out their arms, holding hands. Even though they were hurt and that contact conveyed a bitter pain, it was nice to feel something alive and warm.

«You're a good person, Nivor. I'm glad I made love to you»

Their tears blended on the floor.

Then at once, they closed their eyes. Everything went dark.

«FORGET ABOUT ENDING IT LIKE THIS! YE HAVE NOT SUFFERED ENOUGH YET!»

Aedostul was standing in front of them like a giant. Raising his hand and repeating the gesture, he shot a series of lightning bolts against them.

The first one made them jerk, making their backs snap. All the others had the effect of producing an intense pain that made their senses an unmanageable and unbearable state. If hell existed —they thought— it could not have been much different from what they were experiencing.

Yet Liadra had the lucidity to wonder how anyone could be so mean, especially to their own brother. At that rate, they would have soon made it to the other world.

*** *** ***

In a moment of reprieve, the girl observed Nivor's brother. At that moment, he had two almost squinting eyes. His face looked strangely relaxed; his mouth was slightly open, emulating a sinister smile. Every vein in his body was bulging and protruding, making him resemble a gloomy, creepy freak.

«I have to say that I'm really enjoying my time with you. Ye cannot imagine how good does it feel to eradicate ties to the past. Do ye understand how do I feel right now? The more ye suffer, the happier I am»

Then he approached his brother. He looked down on him with condescension and contempt. With all the strength he had, he began to kick him right in the middle of the stomach. One kick after the other in quick succession.

«THOU ART TRASH TO ME! A USELESS SACK OF SHIT! WHY DIDST THOU HAVE TO EXIST?» he yelled at him.

After all those kicks, Nivor began to emit blood from his mouth; with each blow he spat out a trickle.

Finally, the two victims gave up all resistance and all attachment to life, silently and peacefully resigning themselves to their fate.

«THOU DOST NOT KNOW HOW LONG I HAVE BEEN WAITING FOR THIS MOMENT!» Aedostul said to him, as he continued to kick him.

«I SHALL NEVER FORGET THIS NIGHT. I AM SENDING THEE TO THE NEXT WORLD, THOU SCUM!»

On the one hand, Liadra knew she was about to witness something of inhuman cruelty. On the other, however, she wanted to witness Nivor's last moments.

Suddenly, she noticed something in the background coming into play. Something that Nivor's brother had not calculated on…

Mr. Wakendos, badly torn on the right side of his body, was surreptitiously reaching for Aedostul. When Aedostul realized he was there, it was too late.

Wakendos threw a 5 kg fire extinguisher at Aedostul, thinking it would be enough to knock him out. However, the red metal object simply pierced Aedostul's body and slammed into the ground.

«Here cometh someone I had not expected to see again,» Aedostul said, examining Wakendos. His shoulder was bandaged and he had swabbed part of his neck as best as he could. A boulder must have hit his legs, because he was walking with a bit of a limp.

«How didst thou survive, old man? Shouldn't Stein's bomb have blown thee up?»

«It takes more than that to knock Eugene Wakendos out,» he said

«Nuts. Ye human beings tend to overestimate yourselves»
Because I guess you've stopped being human, haven't you, Nivor Aedostul?»

«My name soundeth a lot better when there's no one around to tarnish it. Anyway, your pathetic fire extinguisher speaketh for itself»

«What have you become, Aedostul? Don't you realize that you have altered the very nature of what makes you human?»

«AND DOST THOU KNOW HOW MUCH DO I CARE ABOUT THAT?! I am immortal this way, I can withstand conditions thou canst not even imagine. Try throwing another fire extinguisher at me, go ahead! I am far better than thy pathetic biological bodies»

«You're a fool, Aedostul. Don't you realize how unnatural this is?»

«Thou art the fool, old man. No one should have bothered me while I was dealing with that louse Stullenbird. Because now I am going to kill thee!»

Aedostul charged Wakendos, once again pulling out his army knife. The scene that followed was heartbreaking. Aedostul began stabbing Wakendos, who was putting up a strenuous resistance.

In the background Liadra whispered to Nivor Stullenbird.

«Fl… flee» she said «Get out of here»

«What good would that do?» he whispered. «I'm about to end up the way I deserve»

«See Nivor… the boy I used to know, wouldn't give himself up to his fate like this, without a fight…», she paused to catch her breath. «In my heart, you're a stupid little head who always does what he wants, even if it's devoid of any logic. If you stay here, not only will you die, but the idea I have of you will die as well…»

«And I will never forgive you for that,» she added.

Stullenbird rested his arm on the puddle of tears and blood that was on the floor; then he levered himself up.

«Aren't you coming?» Nivor asked.

«The bastard's lightning bolts have paralyzed me. I can't do it»

«And how dare you ask me to leave you here!»

«Don't let the idea we all have of you die» Liadra said «Because the idea we have of you is eternal. No matter what happens to us»

Nivor continued to stare at the girl.

«YOU SHOULD HAVE LEFT THE DAMN ETHICS ALONE, OLD MAN! THE BLUE PARTY REACHED THE END OF ITS TETHER A LONG TIME AGO!» Aedostul shouted.

He kept stabbing Wakendos with his knife.After a while all that remained of Wakendos' chest was a shapeless, quartered heap of bloody flesh. From it, gushed a river of blood that stained everything, from Aedostul's suit to the floor, walls and even the ceiling.

*** *** ***

With his wits about him, Aedostul picked up where he left off. He regained his composure, though he was practically stained with blood all over. He looked back at Liadra.

«So, where were we? Oh, yes…»

He froze suddenly at the sight of the floor. There was Liadra; at her side a pile of blood, then a huge clean space.

With all the speed he had, he rushed to her.

«WHERE IS HE!? WHERE HATH HE GONE!?»

Liadra sketched a shy smile

«Who are you talking about?»

«THOU SHALT NOT DARE TEASE ME! WHERE IS STULLENBIRD?»

«Where he has always been» she whispered «In my heart.»

At that point Aedostul got really nervous and emitted a sort of sound, similar to a vowel, which became more and more audible, until it turned into a scream.

With all the strength he had, he plunged the entire blade of the dagger into Liadra's chest. Then he pushed it down, opening it in two and exposing every one of her internal organs to the sunlight.

Nivor Aedostul had killed Liadra

SNOW

From that point on, Nivor Stullenbird would have to fend for himself. Somehow he had regained most of his strength, despite the deep pain in his stomach and his wounds. He focused on his survival, however.

It seemed that the elevator corridor was waiting for no one but him.

On the ceiling, he saw the one-way lights spinning in the very direction he was running, as if to invite him onward.

The corridor was clear of all objects. All the doors to the rooms were closed.

He ran as fast as he could until he reached the call button. He was lucky: the elevator was only on the third floor; so it took it a few seconds to get to the fourth. Seconds, but that seemed like an eternity to Nivor. He swung his feet obsessively looking behind him, afraid that Aedostul would come out from behind the wall. That did not happen, however. The elevator arrived at the floor and the doors opened.

Immediately Nivor stepped into the elevator and pressed the button to the ground floor.

During the descent he had the opportunity to relax and slow down his heartbeat, which went from star-high to "acceptable". He realized he still had Liadra's backpack behind him. It contained not only his belongings, but also those of the girl. With that money and gold, he could have lived more than decently for months.

Finally, after an exhausting wait, the elevator arrived at the ground floor. Not a fly flew there. There was absolute silence. An almost unnatural silence, to be afraid of.

He knew little about alchemy, but he understood that the evil of that night had saturated the place, and would remain there for a long time.

There was no one there but the corpses that Stein and Lightning had left behind. The two killers, however, were on the second floor.

As he walked towards the exit in that silence, Nivor felt a strange sensation. It was like being inside a dream. And for some strange reason, he felt bigger than he was —and he was pretty big.

He could not explain that feeling. It was as if the souls of the innocents killed that night were watching him, as one watches a show, patiently and silently.

In his heart, he wished he did not see any dead bodies —he knew his already tormented stomach could not take it.

At last, he reached the hall, the place where that massacre had started. He could not tell how he had guessed this either —but he knew it. He missed no details; neither Vincent's vacant and bloody guard post, nor the yellowish lights, nor the warm radiators.

Nivor recorded every detail from there on in his mind: the opening of the front door, the squeaky doorknob, the heaviness of the door.

Finally, he left the Atlanta base for ever.

*** *** ***

He was faced with something different from the usual landscape he was accustomed to.

Both the garden and the parking lot had been covered by a thick layer of white. Almost everything was white, with very few exceptions. In the distance, towards the parking lot, he saw a large cloud of black smoke and reddish reflections, as if there was a fire. He wondered what the hell was going on over there. Anyway, it was certainly related to the coup. The snow falling in front of him slowly and quietly, seemed to him to be almost a symbol, marking a break between the hell he left inside the building and the serenity he found outside. Yet he also sensed that he was in a war zone. The atmosphere resulting from the fall of the government — and shortly thereafter, the dissolution of the Parliament— was one of absolute tension.

Quite ahead of the base, on the road, someone had parked a large off-road vehicle, a sort of jeep. There were people inside, because the windshield was clean just following the path of the windshield wiper.

The front passenger door —the one facing the base— opened. A man stepped out. He was of medium height, and was wearing a heavy sweater and glasses, which immediately fogged up on contact with the cold outside.

Nivor stepped back. He had no way of knowing who this strange visitor was. He had parked outside the base right at the end of a massacre; he could be a friend or a foe. Anyway, Nivor could certainly not go back inside, where he would have found madmen on the loose with the stated aim of taking him out. No. He had to stay there and take his chances.

The strange man was about forty years old. He went closer to Nivor.

«What's your name, boy?»

"Who… who is asking?»

«Don't be afraid,» the man said with a smile, «We're scientists. We have nothing in common with extremist forces and we won't do you absolutely any harm»

«My name is Nivor Stullenbird»

At that point, the man suddenly froze. He took off his fogged up glasses and examined Nivor from top to bottom.

«How did you know we were here?» the man asked in curiosity.

«I didn't. In effect, I didn't really understand who you are»

«And how did you escape the DBs and your brother?»

Did he know Aedostul? What the hell was going on?

«It's a long story. Not without pain»

«I see…» the man said, flashing another of his balmy smiles.

«Why don't you get in the car, Nivor? We have a lot of things to talk about»

The whole thing was simply absurd. Under normal circumstances, Nivor would NEVER EVER get into a car that came out of nowhere. Given what happened to him, however, he just didn't want to be there anymore.

A little intimidated —understandably so—, Nivor followed the man, who pointed to the back door.

He opened the door and climbed aboard. Inside it was very well heated and clean, smelling like car air freshener.

The man sat comfortably in the front, on the passenger side.

Behind the wheel was a woman. She was a bit frumpy and thin as well, looking every bit as cultured and serious.

«I was right» the man said. «It's him»

«Then those glasses work» the woman replied. Then she looked back.

«As of now, nice to meet you Nivor. I would have preferred this day to come under slightly different circumstances. However, a few unforeseen events have taken around here, haven't they?»

«Who the hell are you guys?» said Nivor.

The woman sighed. Then she turned back to the front and started the engine.

«We'll explain it to you on the way. But get some rest now. You'll be tired after such a night. If those wounds hurt, there should be a first aid kit back there.»

INTERMISSION

IRON MOUNTAIN, YEAR 12.19.16, DAY 2.1

On the background of a snow-covered valley, two children stood in front of a mountain. You could not have found a better place for skiing, an activity the two brats preferred. Moreover, it was their birthday, so they were allowed to spend the whole day having fun.

«He who arrives last is a rotten fish!» said the boy in the blue coat, as he began his ski descent.

«When I get there, you'll be the rotten fish, Aedostul!» replied the other, who was wearing a bright orange coat.

«Ooh, listen to you! Be careful not to melt the snow with that thing you're wearing, dear Stullenbird!»

The boy in blue was visibly ahead, but both were skiing with absolutely perfect fluidity and agility. They seemed to be in their natural habitat.

They were skiing downhill zigzagging, curving, even looking for ledges, from which to make jumps. Once again, they seemed to have properly tamed their surroundings.

«I'm going to win anyway, Stullenbird!» the child in blue said.

«Yes, but only because you left early, Aedostul! That doesn't count!»

There was someone with the two children: the person who was supervising them. She was a well-hooded woman, who looked horrified and terrified at the two's performance.

«Stop! Stop immediately! This is too dangerous! You're going to get hurt! Come on, get down boys!»

Both children blew a raspberry at the woman, who reacted with a grimace of profound indignation.

They faced a rather difficult and tight curve, but managed to ride it with great agility. They shouted a noisy "WHOO-HOO!"

The speed was increasing at a rapid pace, along with the steepness. The last obstacle was a sort of uphill "rock" covered in snow. The two of them, thanks to their speed, jumped over it and were literally thrown through the air, both ending up, at different times, on the ground.

It was actually not a good landing, but they both had a lot of fun.

Stullenbird's ski came off his foot, while Aedostul lost both his rackets.

«And it's one-nil to Aedostul!» he said happily.

PUAFF.

Immediately, his face got covered in snow.

«Here's your prize! A snowball, you cheater!»

"This is a declaration of war, Stullenbird!»

At that point, they started throwing snowballs at each other, until their clothes were filled with white.

«There you are!» the overseer coming said. «You two, Nivor twins! You are in trouble!»

Without saying a word, the two brothers exchanged a knowing look, almost a bratty smile hinting at their intentions.

PUAFF, PUAFF!

The twins started bombarding their instructor with snowballs. She had no choice but to flee. Then, satisfied with their accomplishment, they laughed at the silly scene they had witnessed. At last, as to end on a high note, they laid down in the snow next to each other.

They began to talk about the friendship they shared. They were happy.

*** *** ***

The structure that housed them was a small base at the foothills of the mountains, in a place where avalanches could not reach. There was a large space at the back, where they used to spend all their time playing and inventing new imaginative things with their friends.

They often played soldiers, pretending to shoot with guns made of paper. Aedostul was better at this game, although Stullenbird always knew how to make himself unpredictable.

«Taking care of those two is pure hell,» their instructor told another colleague. «In no time at all, they take all my life energy.»

«They're twin brothers,» the colleague said. «It's only natural that they'd be in competition with each other.»

«I wonder if they'll grow up and get along so well. Those two together are dangerous.»

The woman, however, had already stopped paying attention to her colleague.

«Stullenbird, Aedostul, leave those plants alone! Woe betide you if I find even a speck of soil lying around!»

The twins took off running.

«It is really impossible to deal with those two boys. They always find a mess to make»

«Yet I think they are destined to do great things one day. It's written in their future»

«Yes, I know. They have immense potential. Too bad that right now they only use that potential to create confusion»

At meal times, the twins always used to seat side by side. No matter how hard the instructors tried to pull them apart, they were inseparable in every sense of the word.

With them around, every meal almost always ended up turning into a food fight, where they used their spoons as slingshots to throw all sorts of food at each other. This time was different, as their favorite dishes had been prepared for the occasion: mushroom fettuccine for Stullenbird and salmon penne for Aedostul.

«Are we already 9 years old?» Stullenbird asked to his brother.

«No, we'll turn them at midnight,» Aedostul replied.

«Why at midnight? It's not like we were born at that time»

«It's one of those things that adults do»

«I hope they don't sing us that nasty little song»

«Really! That would be super-duper embarrassing!»

The twins began talking about many other things.

*** *** ***

Then they spent the rest of the afternoon playing video games.

The formula was always the same: they would sit on the floor in front of the console with the controllers in their hands and stare at the screen. As long as they were playing, the world could have fallen, they would not have noticed anything. Everything was put in the background.

At that moment, they were playing a classic car racing game. Of course, for them the competition was at its peak. Both were aiming for victory, even if they often ended their matches in draws. Anyway, they used to get the highest scores among all the players in the base.

That day, they also managed to make an usual trouble of theirs. Stullenbird was peeing in the toilet, when suddenly Aedostul bursted in with a giant fish —at least compared to the two kids. He had stolen it from the canteen freezer.

«Look, Stullenbird, I found someone who likes you!» said Aedostul, as he manipulated the poor fish's lips.

«Where did you even get that thing?»

«He wants to get with you! Look!» and always moving the fish's mouth with his fingers, he "made" it say yes.

Then Aedostul threw the fish to Stullenbird, who having good coordination, caught it on the fly. Then he threw it back at Aedostul, and that's when they started playing catch... with a cod.

After a dozen shots, the fish slipped from Stullenbird's hands and plummeted straight into the toilet.

101

«What do we do now?» he asked his brother.

«Take it easy» said Aedostul calmly, «It will go away,» and he flushed.

But the fish did not go away. On the contrary, the water rose to the surface and the fish remained clogged in the pipe.

At that point, the two of them ran out of the bathroom before anyone discovered what they had done.

Over the course of the day, they were terrified that someone would discover the trouble they had made. Fortunately, however, everything went smoothly. As a consequence, they finally concluded that the fish had gone into the pipes.

At nine o'clock in the evening, however things suddenly changed. They had just finished their dinner, and were waiting for the cake, when an instructor approached them with a heavy step and an angry look.

«YOU TWO!» he yelled. «Who's been? One of you has clogged the toilet bowl with a sea bass! Who?»

They pointed at each other. «Him!». «Him!» they said with one voice.

«What did they do!?» asked the woman

«I have just noticed that the toilet was clogged. I looked closer, and there was a fish tail under there! Crazy stuff!»

«You need to compliment the cleaners and tell them that fish grew in the toilet,» Stullenbird muttered.

«DOES THAT SOUND LIKE FUN TO YOU?» the woman screamed.

Luckily for them, it was their birthday, so that they were not punished for their stunt. The incident was glossed over, and the adults made an effort to see the comical side of the situation.

Finally, the cake arrived, and the two blew out the candles together. It had been an absolutely wonderful double birthday.

INTERMISSION ENDS

NIVOR STULLENBIRD CEASES EXISTING

Nivor Stullenbird woke up slowly and remained for a while quietly in bed. He had fallen asleep on the jeep ride, and still needed to get his energy back. His body was still sore from the kicks and other blows he had taken from Aedostul, but healing processes had already been activated.

He looked around. He was in some sort of infirmary, but it certainly was not the one in Atlanta base. Too bad, he had hoped that the events of the night before would turn out to be just a bad nightmare.

The same man who had accompanied him there approached him very calmly.

«How are you, Nivor?»

«I'm fine… I guess…» he said. Actually, a flurry of questions were swirling in his head.

«Where am I?»

«You're in Iron Muntain»

That name was not new to him.

«What time is it?»

«7:30. It's been twenty-four hours since the coup»

With much effort, he tried to get up. He was barefoot, but at the side of the bed he saw his shoes and a pair of slippers.

«I remember this place. This is where my brother and I grew up»

103

«That's right» said the man

«So you must be one of my old instructors»

«That's right again»

«What happened in Atlanta?»

The man seemed to hesitate before answering «When the police raided the building, they were already gone. I don't know the details, but they said they'd never seen a massacre like that»

«How's Liadra? Is she safe?»

"She's probably on an autopsy table now.»

«No… all this wasn't supposed to happen»

"Do you wonder, Nivor? It was a tragedy foretold»

«My brother… He's responsible»

«I know» the man said

«That's why you're here»

«What have I to do with him?»

«You get dressed" he told him «I'll be back in five minutes»

Thus said, the man left with his usual serenity.

Nivor spent that time trying to get up, put his clothes back on and try to walk again. He was still in a lot of pain, so it was no surprise that he limped badly. In effect, every single step stung like hell. There was such a silence, however, and he began to reflect on the events that had occurred.

*** *** ***

A short while later, the man came back. He nodded to Nivor to invite him follow him.

«I don't understand what you're trying to get with me» he said «I don't know anything about my brother's business»

«I know, Nivor, I know. Don't worry»

They had started down some spiral stairs. Nivor had to strain a little to keep from stumbling.

«The world is in serious trouble, Nivor. Your brother and the DBs are close to coming to power. Both the Government and the Parliament have fallen»

«I used to know my brother was crazy, but I didn't imagine to this extent. You know… that he would go this far just for power»

«What your brother is following, is a strong mechanistic ideology. He intends to convert every person into a machine. This is the most extreme side of the polarization of order»

«I don't understand much about alchemy» Nivor said.

Meanwhile, the two of them were heading underground.

«You know that as twins, you and your brother have the same DNA, don't you?»

Nivor nodded.

«And do you also know that you two were not born… let's say by the natural method? Do you know you are true genetic engineering projects?»

«What are you getting at?»

«You and your brother have great power. Your DNA gives you abilities beyond all limits, both intellectually, physically, and especially alchemically»

«So far, he's always been the more advanced one. I've always been thinking about… having fun»

«The point, is that he now has all the credentials to fulfill his ends, which translate into his ambition to dominate the world. Have you ever heard the expression "new world order"?»

«Yeah… from some plotters»

«That's exactly what the DBs intend to create»

«This is going from bad to worse,» Nivor said dejectedly.

«Besides, your brother is looking for you in every corner of the world. He's given every DB a mandate to take you out, should you be spotted»

«Yesterday he tried to kill me»

«And for good reason, according to his point of view. You see, since you have the same genetic code, everything he can do, you could do too, if you had his means»

They stopped in front of a room. Inside, there was a huge vertical tube made of glass, a sort of capsule.

«But I don't have» Nivor was examining the room they had arrived in. Next to the capsule, there was a large computer that looked really advanced and incredibly full of different keys.

«Life is not like video games, Nivor» the man said «There is no way to start the game over once you get into an unpleasant situation»

«You can say that!» he added «If I had the chance, I would stop at nothing to prevent my brother from reaching his evil goals»

«In the whole world, Nivor, there's no one more likely to succeed than you»

«But I don't see how!» he shouted «He's going to rule the world… he's got an indestructible body… he's going to win the elections soon… and everyone wants me dead. How do I tick off this situation?»

«There is a way» the man replied «That's why I brought you here»

«Before I tell you, answer me. Are you absolutely willing to stop your brother?»

«I will. Even at the cost of my own life. Only I can do it»

«Hear hear! Well then» the man said «Do you see that capsule in the back there?» and saying so, he pointed to the large vertical glass tube. Nivor nodded,

«It is a device that the Blue Party has been secretly developing. It can change your identity… I mean, totally. Once you go in there, you come out an entirely different person»

«Crap! That's exactly what I need!»

«Don't be too happy, Nivor. See, such a procedure has two major flaws»

«Yeah, fuck… It seemed too good to be true. Go on, tell me. What those flaws are?»

«First one: it takes a long time. I felt free to perform some simulations… in your case, the process will take no less than fifteen years»

«SO I WILL GET OUT OF THERE IN 15 FUCKING YEARS?»

«And that is only the lesser evil. Then comes the second problem.»

In order to better explain, the man pulled out a nametag from his lab coat. On it, a name Nivor had never heard.

«Who is this Dylan Near?» he asked, curious.

«Due to a series of alchemical distortions, as I was saying…» said the man «…Those who enter here lose all memories. Completely»

«What kind of memories?»

«Everything. Everything that is traceable to this life. A veritable "veil of forgetfulness", we could say. You'll forget your current identity, the things you've done, even your name. And certainly also that you are Aedostul's brother»

«Will I forget the Atlanta massacre as well?»
The man nodded.

«So, if I understand correctly, when I get out of there in 15 years, I won't know who I am, my name'll be Dylan Near, I'll live in an unknown world, and I'll be tasked with stopping my brother —which I'll not know is my brother anymore? Am I right?»

«You'd still have your soul, Nivor. It's true that you would become a different person in every way, but your soul and your DNA wouldn't change at all. And consider that there are some positive aspects to it as well»

«Meaning?»

«First, you'll hardly age. Once you get out of there you'll barely be twenty. Second —IF and I repeat IF— Dylan will have the desire to do this, he'll be able to retrieve your memories»

Nivor thought carefully about these words. At the implications they carried. He —in the sense of who he was at that moment— would have to die and be reborn in the form of another person: Dylan Near. He would have no way of knowing that his name used to be Nivor or that he was

Aedostul's brother. He would have no memory of his experiences in Atlanta, but neither would he have any memory of the massacre that took place there.

Nivor thought about the future. What would the world have looked like in 15 years? It would have been a new place, completely different from the one he used to know. That was for sure.

Would Aedostul finally rise to power? How would he —or rather, Dylan— live in a world he did not know, and without any memories? In a world full of technologies he did not even dream of?

«There's no shortage of doubts» Nivor muttered. «But I accept»

The scientist performed the procedure to open the capsule. Nivor entered the glass cylinder. Then, the scientist closed and sealed it operating with the computer. Finally, the capsule was filled with liquid nitrogen, freezing Nivor.

When he got out of there, he would be called Dylan Near. He would not know he used to be Aedostul's brother, nor would he have any memory of his previous life. But he would be tasked with stopping him, no matter what world he landed in.

«Goodbye Nivor… or rather… Dylan… See you in the future!» the man finally said.

The real story commences now.

THE END